P9-DDC-169

CHASE BRANCH LIBRARY
1 731 W. SEVEN MILE RD.
DETROIT, MI 48235
578-8002

NOV 09

CH

BLACK
ANGELS

BY THE AUTHOR OF

Crossing Over Jordan

BLACK ANGELS

LINDA BEATRICE BROWN

G. P. Putnam's Sons • Penguin Young Readers Group

G. P. PUTNAM'S SONS
A division of Penguin Young Readers Group.
Published by The Penguin Group.
Penguin Group (USA) Inc., 375 Hudson Street, New York, NY 10014, U.S.A.
Penguin Group (Canada), 90 Eglinton Avenue East, Suite 700, Toronto, Ontario M4P 2Y3,
Canada (a division of Pearson Penguin Canada Inc.).
Penguin Books Ltd, 80 Strand, London WC2R 0RL, England.
Penguin Ireland, 25 St. Stephen's Green, Dublin 2, Ireland (a division of Penguin Books Ltd.).
Penguin Group (Australia), 250 Camberwell Road, Camberwell, Victoria 3124, Australia
(a division of Pearson Australia Group Pty Ltd).
Penguin Books India Pvt Ltd, 11 Community Centre, Panchsheel Park,
New Delhi - 110 017, India.
Penguin Group (NZ), 67 Apollo Drive, Rosedale, North Shore 0632, New Zealand
(a division of Pearson New Zealand Ltd).
Penguin Books (South Africa) (Pty) Ltd, 24 Sturdee Avenue, Rosebank,
Johannesburg 2196, South Africa.
Penguin Books Ltd, Registered Offices: 80 Strand, London WC2R 0RL, England.

Copyright © 2009 by Linda Beatrice Brown
All rights reserved. This book, or parts thereof, may not be reproduced in any form without
permission in writing from the publisher, G. P. Putnam's Sons, a division of Penguin Young
Readers Group, 345 Hudson Street, New York, NY 10014.
G. P. Putnam's Sons, Reg. U.S. Pat. & Tm. Off. The scanning, uploading and distribution
of this book via the Internet or via any other means without the permission of the publisher is
illegal and punishable by law. Please purchase only authorized electronic editions, and do not
participate in or encourage electronic piracy of copyrighted materials. Your support
of the author's rights is appreciated. The publisher does not have any control over and
does not assume any responsibility for author or third-party websites or their content.
Published simultaneously in Canada.
Printed in the United States of America.
Design by Marikka Tamura.
Text set in Kennerly.
Library of Congress Cataloging-in-Publication Data.
Brown, Linda Beatrice, 1939-
Black angels / by Linda Beatrice Brown. p. cm.
Summary: Three Southern children, two black and one white, escape from their homes
during the horrors of the Civil War and, after meeting in the woods, gradually come to rely on
each other as they make their way slowly north, enduring hunger, fear, sickness,
and constant danger, before arriving in Harper's Ferry, West Virginia.
[1. Coming of age—Fiction. 2. Survival—Fiction. 3. Race relations—Fiction.
4. United States—History—Civil War, 1861–1865—Fiction. 5. African Americans—Fiction.
6. Indians of North America—Fiction. 7. Southern States—History—1775–1865—Fiction.
8. Southern States—History—1865–1877—Fiction.] I. Title.
PZ7.B816138BI 2009 [Fic]—dc22 2008049244
ISBN 978-0-399-25030-9
1 3 5 7 9 10 8 6 4 2

To My Mother, Edith Brown

1907–1999

Who Taught Me to Love the Imagination

and

To My Father, Raymond Brown

1907–1998

Who Taught Me to Love Freedom

CHAPTER 1

LUKE
THE EAGLE

Luke took the key out of the sideboard drawer in the dining room, took a rifle and put the key back very carefully. The drawer stuck so he couldn't get it closed. It squeaked slightly. If he forced it, it would jar the whole rifle case. He breathed short, shallow breaths and felt his heartbeat shaking his entire chest. How would he ever get the drawer shut without being heard? If they saw it open, they'd notice the missing gun for sure.

He pushed gently. The sideboard rattled. The drawer still wouldn't give. Lord, someone would be hearing him. He pushed one more time, and the drawer went in with a click that was as loud as a gunshot to him. But he had the rifle! The powder bag was in his pocket.

He hung Massa's tin box with its flint and steel for making fires around his neck in its little bag. Massa had already eaten. He'd be sleeping it off now, gone in early for the night. And Eugenia would be fixing their supper. They always had to wait and eat whatever was left over.

Luke would eat supper and pretend everything was normal. Then he'd wait until it got good and late before he left. By the time he was missed, it would be morning and they wouldn't know where to start looking. If he could just make his way out of the house tonight without being seen.

Supper was butter beans and corn and a little piece of pork chop Aunt Eugenia had saved for him. Massa always said he was fattening Luke up for special work. He'd be special and never have to fear being sold away. Luke didn't really taste his food though. He could hardly stand the excitement, knowing it was his last meal at that kitchen table; he might never see Aunt Eugenia again. His stomach was jumping like a wild thing, but he tried hard to act normal because Aunt Eugenia could smell mischief a mile away.

He wiped grease out from under his lip. She made him clean his plate and wash it at the pump, looking at him sideways with her forehead wrinkled up, like she knew he was up to something. When he came back in, the one kerosene lamp was shining on her dark brown face. The way she licked her lips, he knew what was coming.

Finally she said it. "Ain't no sense you thinking bout running."

Luke jumped.

"Them Yankees have you snatched up in a minute. Eat you alive."

"Yes, ma'am," Luke said. But he thought, Old ladies always scared. Yankees can't be that bad.

"And go get me some wood for the stove, and put them rakes away fore too late. Us got a early morning comin. Need to get to bed. Missus want a big breakfast for company. Don't know what they spect me to use for provisions. Us running outta everything. Dadblast Yankees anyhow. They ain't no better'n any other White folks. Lord, she want light bread. Got to get up fore day in morning." She groaned and slid back her chair. "Blow out the lamp after you lays that fire for mornin, Luke, I'm dead." Tired, she slammed the kitchen door and walked off into the gloom toward her cabin. It was close to the kitchen so she could be called during the night.

Luke couldn't believe his luck. She had left him alone to finish up. She'd never done that before. She must have been really worn out. Now he could find some food to take with him. He finished his chores and looked around the kitchen. There was some corn bread left, but that was all. He'd have to find more than that.

A streak of lightning lit up the northern sky. He went to his pallet in the fruit cellar next to the kitchen where he slept. He guessed a little rest would be good before he started on the road north, but he dozed fitfully. He kept falling asleep and waking up, and finally he couldn't stand it any longer, so he sat up listening for sounds.

Something creaked. A rumble of thunder far away. He guessed the others must have left by now.

Luke opened the door a crack. No moon. It was completely dark. He reckoned it would take him an hour to get to the place. They were set to meet at the place where three big trees were growing together. It was called the haints' place. Luke knew what that meant, that spirits were there. He didn't like that, but he thought it'd be all right. By then the moon would be up and they'd be together. Him and Gustavus, Unc Steph and Junior Boy. He couldn't let them see him coming. They weren't taking children under fifteen. But if he met them, they'd have no choice but to take him along.

Unc Steph would be right proud of him. He had him a prize too. One of Massa's rifles! "My man," that's what Unc Steph would say. "That's what I call a right grown man!"

Luke would be twelve on his next birthday. Or that's what he counted up. Nobody knew for sure how long ago he'd been born.

Luke looked around the fruit cellar. There was only a dim light cast from the kitchen fireplace. It threw a glow onto the dried apples for pies, and peppers on a string. He'd heard Eugenia talking about hiding food yesterday, so they wouldn't starve if the Yankees come. He decided to take apples and raisins, and from the bread box, more of yesterday's corn bread. He wrapped it in a napkin and stuffed it in his shirt, then saw a knife on the windowsill that Aunt Eugenia had forgot to put away. He stared at it, thought "yes," finally, and grabbed it.

Luke stepped out of the back door into the night. He wiped his hand across his eyes. There was no way he could have told her good-bye. She would have stopped him sure enough. He wished he didn't care. He wished he didn't love nobody. Always somebody to say good-bye to.

Crickets whined, and it was so humid you could feel damp on your skin. Hot and damp. September summer.

Something fluttered in the dark and startled him. Maybe it was a bat. He walked quickly around to the side porch, carefully stepping over branches that would crack. The rifle was there, under the porch where he'd hidden it, half wrapped in the buckram. He tucked it tightly under his arm. Now he had to make it off the place without Massa's three-legged hunting dog, Black Nigger, turning up, or worse. He could go through the trees to the back pasture and over the fence to the road. Frogs sang. They sounded louder to him than he'd ever heard them.

He climbed the pasture fence easily, dropping down softly on the other side. The road to the river should be very close. As he neared the road, a loud thunderclap surprised him, and Luke turned to see the brilliant streak of light in the sky. It was right over Massa's house. In the bright flash he saw the rocking chairs on the wraparound porch sway a little in the breeze and the two old pecan trees in the yard where he had picked up so many buckets of pecans for Aunt Eugenia's pies. The trees were tall, old and gnarled, but they grew lots of pecans. In the distance, he could just barely see the cabins where the field hands lived. The rain had finally started. Luke adjusted his food bundle to keep it dry and was on his way.

CHAPTER 2

LEFT BEHIND

It drizzled just a little at first, white flashes of light overhead, and a few drops. Luke padded along quickly on the muddy road. It had wagon ruts in it where water was collecting from the rain. Soon he left the road and crossed what he thought was Black Ankle Creek. The creek was supposed to be good luck, that's what Gustavus had told him. Black ankles crossing the creek meant you were on your way north.

He was moving faster now. It wouldn't do to be caught. He was more afraid of that than he was of being out here in the woods at night, or rebs or Yankees or anything.

Massa Higsaw was bad with runaways, and he had been in a bad mood what with the war he said "messin up his life." It wouldn't do to be caught, not at all. War or no war, proclamation or no proclamation. Massa Higsaw didn't care what Lincoln said.

Suddenly the rain came on hard and fast. Luke was trying to see his way clear to the place where haints came out at night—that's where they were meeting—but it was hard going with the rain beating down on him. In a few minutes, he was soaking wet. The soles of his shoes were soggy, and his bread and fruit would be too wet now. He'd have to give in and stop, find a place to stay until it let up some.

Luke had been this far away before, hunting with Massa, and he thought he knew of a place near here where a big boulder formed a kind of shelter. He'd have to go a little deeper into the woods to find it. But things looked strange in the darkness. If he could find it, he could get under the edge of the boulder and stay dry for a while.

It was winter when he was here before. Now the trees were thick with leaves. He was looking for a big crooked rock that stuck out from the hill. It had scrubby plants around it. The mud and leaves were almost covering his feet. He was ready to give up when he turned to the right and saw the place. It was pretty dry under there.

This wasn't good; he hadn't counted on rain. What if they had decided to go another night on account of the rain? It kept up lightning and thundering. Luke shuddered. He wished he had a quilt, but that was too much to be dragging along. He was not sure he could catch up with the others now, especially if they didn't stop for the rain.

Gradually the rain slowed down, the thunder moved off. Luke got to his feet. Which way now, which way to the haints' place? He looked around, trying to be sure he was walking in the right direction. It all looked the same in the dark, as if the leaves had closed behind him. He thought he had been more than halfway there before he stopped. But the more he looked, the more he didn't know for sure.

It was darker than the devil's mouth. When the moon broke through the clouds, he knew how late it was. He chose left, and set out through the wet underbrush, praying he was going the right way. Soon he saw the river again, and he knew he was right. But he didn't see nobody. This was the place. The river water was as shiny as Miz Higsaw's black silk dress. He could see little squints of light where the moon touched the water. The river was full of all that rain that had come down. And the big trees stood there like giant soldiers.

This was the place where haints was "subject to fix" you unless you had your mojo. Luke wore one around his neck. It was his mam's charm. Where could they be? He made the dove's sound, a signal from slave to slave on the run. Maybe they couldn't hear him over the sound of the river. Maybe they were hiding. And maybe he was just too late.

He made the sound again. Nothing. Ain't nobody here, he thought finally. They done left me. All there is to it. They done left me at the place where the haints get you. Tears filled his eyes and spilled over. He didn't care. Nobody here to see him crying.

Rain dripped off the trees. It was still coming down a bit. He heard an owl, and the moon outlined the footprints he had made in the mud. He had stuck the butt of his rifle in the muck, buckram and all, and he leaned on it, wiping his eyes with his wet sleeve. His stomach growled and turned inside out. But he didn't feel hungry, not even a little bit.

They were going north, he knew that. He ought to try to figure out which way was north by the stars. He'd follow the river away from home. This was North Carolina, and the river should take him to Virginia. He knew about that from Unc Steph. Owls hooted, but he didn't hear any sounds people would make. He was sure to be in these woods alone.

He'd have to work his way back to the road. It was close; he'd just have to turn the right way, and he'd see the road soon. Leaves were mushy under his feet. He had goose bumps

from the cold. His shirt stuck to him. It was very dark for a
while when the moon went under the clouds. Finally the trees
thinned and he was back on the muddy road. His heart lifted
a little. Maybe he didn't need the others anyway.

Luke walked until dawn. At least he could see where he
was going. The damp air was much cooler than it was last
night. He heard birds calling to each other from the trees. If
the sun came out, it would warm him up, and maybe he could
dry out a little bit. He knew his gunpowder might not be dry,
but he was too tired to think about it. He walked until the sun
was up far enough for him to know it would be a nice day.

Up ahead was a big old pine with branches that reached out
and hung down, almost to the ground. It was off the road, and
he could curl up on the east side of the tree and be easily
missed by a passerby. Pine needles make a soft bed, he thought.
Maybe it wouldn't be too wet under the tree. It was the
best he could do. Maybe he'd be safe here. He slept heavy, wet
and all.

• • •

*"You seven," she said. "Seven big years old, and you still with
me. Ain't lost you yet. I ain't had my baby sold away all these
seven years. That be good luck, Luke, good luck. Seven a good
number." He couldn't see her face, only her hands and her apron,
blue and white flowers. Her voice made him feel good though. He
liked it, but something about it hurt him too . . . and then it was
another voice, saying, "Please, Massa, no, Massa, please, it
ain't for me, Massa, spare my boy, Massa, he just a innocent
chile, ain't planned no escape, only us'n, spare my baby, he
don't know nothing" . . . and the voice he heard hurt him, hurt
him so bad, like a terrible knife in his ears it hurt him, and there
was just awful loud screaming, a whip crack and screaming . . . ,*

and then the voice stopped, and he saw his mama's red back in
the dust.

Luke sat straight up with the sun in his face. He had that
dream a lot, and he hated it. He guessed the devil was after
him with that dream. Luke felt for his rifle and heard his stomach growl. He thought about Aunt Eugenia's biscuits and molasses. Maybe he should go back. But then he thought about
being whipped for running away. Whatever happened, it
couldn't be as bad as the whipping. Even Yankees couldn't be
that bad. Luke searched in his shirt for the food he had wrapped
in the napkin. It was soggy, but he ate it anyway, and set out
to go north, on the river road.

CHAPTER 3

DAYLILY
THE BEAR

Daylily couldn't feel her hands. They were there and then they were gone. She didn't know where. There was just cold where she thought her hands should be. They cut Buttercup's babies. Did they cut off her hands too? She didn't remember. Daylily started to shake. Maybe she'd never stop shaking.

Buttercup wasn't shaking any more. Daylily thought, if she stopped shaking, maybe she would be like Buttercup; she'd be dead. Maybe she'd go to Heaven if she died. Maybe she'd have a home in the kingdom like the preacher said.

She couldn't shut her eyes; she knew that. If she shut them, she'd see it again. Those big men with the whiskers. And Buttercup's arms and legs kicking like a scared chicken. And the babies screaming. She'd see it all over again, and then she'd pee in her drawers again. There was only dark in front of her eyes now; those men had gone away a long time ago.

She wanted a drink so much her tongue stuck to the inside of her mouth. Granny used to give her water from a dipper. Granny was dead.

Them soldiers was comin. Yankee soldiers. Everybody say they was gon be free. She remembered everybody was hollering and some running. Clearing out fore the Yankees come. Yankees be burning things, taking what they wanted. Then Granny died. Buttercup died. No, the bad soldiers killed her. Missus was right. She say Yankees from the devil. They do bad things and they kill. She reckoned the ones who killed Buttercup were Yankees. But maybe they was just bad mens.

It started raining and they said some bad words, and then they took the mules and wagon and cut out. There was no light out here. If the moon came out, Daylily would see. Buttercup was lying over there. She hoped the moon didn't come out.

But if the moon did come out, she could make her way to the water and not fall on Buttercup. She could see snakes too if they wasn't asleep in the leaves. They was probably asleep. Maybe it was the wrong time of year for snakes to be out. Maybe they'd be sleep. Maybe.

Daylily was afraid. Granny said, "Sing, can't be afraid if you sing." But the sickness came and got Granny. Her eyes was open too. Rolled back in her head like two glass balls. Her arm twitched.

Granny had said, "Sing, gal. It keep you strong. Sing bout them angels in the White folks' church. They be flyin roun. Us Black folks, we don't fly nowhere, we just work till we die. Preacher say we gon have wings too. Well, we'll see. You go on now, gal, you fly away. You be free for Granny."

Maybe Granny was right. If she would sing, maybe she wouldn't be so afraid. She tried to make a noise come out. Then she felt the hard roots of the big tree under her behind, and that broke something she had been holding on to.

She shifted her weight. Her body hurt everywhere. The clouds had moved too, and the moonlight finally broke into the woods. Her mouth opened just a little. She wouldn't turn her head though. Buttercup was there. Right there.

"Mama, are there angels . . . ," she tried to sing, but no sound came out.

Daylily thought it silently in her head, the way Granny used to sing it. "Mama, are there any angels Black like . . . Black like me? I've been as good as any little girl can be. If I hide my face, do you think they will see? Mama, are there any angels Black like me?"

The leaves rustled a little in the wind. Buttercup was there, right by the water. You can't be scared if you sing. In her head she could hear the tune just a little. The song came out a tiny bit like a sick kitten she'd seen once down by the big house, mewing for its mama. And then more of it came out. She sang, "I have been as good as any little girl can be . . ."

The moon was shining on the running creek. Maybe they'd come back. They'd stuck Buttercup with a knife like she was a pig, and left her dead. Daylily's throat hurt. She was so thirsty. She could tell by the quiet of the woods that it would soon be morning. Soon be day. And she'd have to see her, even if she didn't go get some water. And she'd have to remember it all.

It was there in her head. The big men and the wagon they took. She could hear it. She could still hear the babies scream- ing for they mama. She started singing to cover up the sound in her head. "If I hide my face, do you think they will see . . ." But she remembered Buttercup's face was all twisted. Butter- cup tried to hide herself. She tried, but they tore off her dress anyway; the babies was dead then.

Daylily guessed one man covered them up with his big

hands so they couldn't holler and couldn't breathe, and they was dead, and Buttercup was all full of blood and spread open like a hog, like a brown and red hog on the ground.

They didn't know Daylily was hiding, right there where she still was, cause Buttercup fell to fighting so hard. When they wasn't looking, Daylily got up from the wagon bed and stole away. But she saw it behind a bunch of blackberry bushes and honeysuckle vines all knotted up. It was getting on to dark fast, but she saw it. One had red hair. A big beard.

When they left the home place, Buttercup was going to find her man. Two plantations to the north, she said. War done come. They was free, she said. Her man was free. Was they flying around free now? Daylily wondered. Was Buttercup and her babies free angels?

"Are there any angels Black like me?" the song said. Her small, high voice took up very little space. "I have been as good as any little girl can be." She could feel her hands now. They were tingling. She could see the water move in the gray light. "If I hide my face, do you think they will see? Mama, are there any angels Black like me?"

Just one or two steps and she'd be there. She'd step over the other way, away from where she knew Buttercup was left by the bad men, and she wouldn't turn her head. Just a drink. A swallow.

She was there and she bent over on her knees and drank. It was a cold, dark feeling, but it was good.

She turned around, not really seeing anything clearly, but heading away from the water some, and as far away from the bodies as she could manage. She was already half asleep, and damp with last night's rain. She was very, very sleepy, and she closed her eyes tight, feeling the crying come on her.

She heard a wood thrush in a tree somewhere. Its partner answered. A squirrel stirred and buzzards circled overhead. It tasted like salt water was running down her face and under her chin. Dew formed its tiny bubbles. It would be a fine September morning.

CHAPTER 4

CASWELL
THE WOLF

He only had to find her. He only had to reach the Burwell place and she would be there. It was late afternoon now. Daniel taught him about the sun and how to read it. Before he got to the Burwell place, he'd have to wash his face. He was a big boy, seven years old. He had no business crying. Mamadear would die if she knew how filthy he was. He thought his face was probably black with grime and his trousers looked like niggers' trousers, covered with mud and dust.

His papa was away fighting Yankees, a brave and true son of the Confederacy, and he had no business crying like a girl. Not ever. No excuse for it. Caswell wiped his eyes with the back of his hand. Now he was on the river road. He knew that he was right because he knew the river road ran down to the Burwell place. He was on the river road cause he had to find his Mamadear.

When Papa went off to war, Caswell remembered he could not cry, and so he ran off down near the pond to wash his face quick, and Sweetbriar saw him and said, "Yo daddy whup you for blubberin, Marse Caswell?"

"Shut up, you nigger, you just shut up," he told Sweet-briar.

It was summertime when Papa left. Magnolias were out full, and tobacco was high and green, and Mama was big in the stomach. She was bigger than he'd ever seen her, and Sweetbriar said, "Them's two melons your mama got in her belly. She get small again, you see. And then you have two little bundles in your house."

And then Sweetbriar had to go cause Gran Susie called him to fetch her water, but Caswell's mama didn't ever get small again, and Papa went off to fight.

Now he was by himself. But he knew he was going the right way because his papa had taken him to the Burwell place. They got in the buggy and General Brown drove them there behind Blue Sam and Soldier Boy, Papa's new geldings. He wanted to show Colonel Burwell his new horses, he said. Show him what a real gentleman would have. They went on a long time in the buggy, and he heard Papa say, "General Brown, how far you reckon Burwell's is?"

General Brown said, "Bout ten miles, Marse Washington."

"Nonsense," Papa said. "It's no ten miles. Seven at the most. You boys just don't have a head for these things." Papa laughed.

"Yessuh," General Brown said, like he always did. And clucked the horses to speed up.

Papa said General Brown wasn't really a general, but he gave him that name because he liked to joke with his friends when they visited that he had a retired general on the place, and then he'd call General Brown in to serve the drinks and they'd all laugh.

At the Burwell place they'd talk about how brave Caswell

was and call him a little man. He felt bad though. Papa said he had to be the man on the place, and he'd let Papa down. He couldn't stop the burning. He'd let Mamadear down too. All her beautiful things were gone.

If he could just find a way to wash his face, so they wouldn't know he had cried. He gazed at the riverbank. It looked pretty steep to him. He could wash his face in the river, but he might slip and fall and then his pants would get all wet and muddy. Maybe he'd try later.

Mama had swooned the day Papa marched off to war. Ladies did those things. She had cried all morning. She had wiped her eyes and lay down with a sick headache and took camphor all day. Then they came for Papa, and she got up and went downstairs to see him off, leaning on Gran Susie's arm.

Papa kissed her on the cheek so it'd be seemly and marched off with the Thirty-first. So she was standing in front of the gate when she swooned, and everybody ran to pick her up off the ground. Gran Susie yelled to get her salts and a cool cloth and water, and she said, "You, Daniel, carry the missus to her room!"

Papa had on a gray uniform, and he said the Thirty-first was a grand group of men. Caswell was going to join them when he grew up, he knew that. But then after Papa marched away, he ran off cause he was a coward who had to cry.

His face hurt now and his feet too. He was awfully tired of the river road, and it was hard to remember where he was. He had walked two miles at least. But he didn't see any houses or any people or lights. It was dark enough to see lights now. He was hungry, really hungry. Maybe he should stop and eat the bread he had brought with him.

They'd have food at the Burwells'. Lots of good food like

before. Chicken and jams, jellies and ice cream. He could eat some more when he got there.

He wanted his Mamadear. He wanted his bed. He wanted Gran Susie. He'd lie down, that's what. He'd been out here for so long. He could leave the river road just long enough to rest a few minutes. He wanted his bread now.

Caswell walked a few more minutes into the woods, and then he fell forward on his knees, taking the bread out of his shirt. He remembered that Mamadear fell down too. She had come out into the yard where he was. She was sweating. He had never seen her sweat before. Only niggers sweated, she said. But then she did, and she fell down on her knees, and said over and over, "Call someone, Caswell, be a good boy and call someone. Get Gran Susie. The baby's comin'."

He didn't know what to do and he didn't know where Gran Susie was, or where General Brown was, so he went off to find Daniel. He couldn't even find Sweetbriar, and then he began to cry, before he heard the hoofbeats.

He remembered a rider coming, and there was dust everywhere, and he stopped in front of their yard looking wild and saying something about Yankee soldiers burning, on the way, and niggers on the loose, get out now. And then he said, "My God, what's going on?"

Mama said real weak-like, "Get me to the Burwell place, they got protection."

The rider said, "Don't you have a nigger?"

"I don't know. I guess they are all out back. My husband is off at the war," Mama shouted.

"I've got to water my horse, ma'am or he'll die; I been whupping him to death," the rider said.

Then Mama screamed. "Get somebody!" she said.

So Caswell ran down to the barn looking for Gran Susie, who wasn't in the house or anywhere else he could find. He remembered it all now.

The bread Daniel found was good. Gran Susie's bread was always good. She was gone though. Daniel said, "They's all gone, Marse Caswell." So he ran back to the house as fast as he could with Daniel limping behind him. And when Caswell got back to the house, Mamadear was not there and he couldn't find her.

That was yesterday. Now he was lost in the woods. He wouldn't cry. He wouldn't be such a baby. When the rider left, and Mamadear was gone and General Brown and Gran Susie, it was just him and Daniel on the whole place.

He had to find Mamadear. Sweetbriar could have helped. He was good at some things even if he was a nigger. Papa would whip him for leaving, and Gran Susie, who Mamadear said was her best friend, even if she was black as a swamp. Papa would whip them good when he came back. He was right, you had to keep niggers in line.

He wanted a knife. No, a sword would be better, like the one his daddy said General Robert E. Lee carried. The one he saw in the picture book. The bread he had eaten made a heavy lump in his stomach. He wanted a drink. Then he wanted to relieve himself. It took a long time for him to unbutton his pants. He looked around. It was almost completely dark. He went a few feet from the clearing where he had stopped, and squatted. In his mind he saw his Mamadear kneeling on the ground. It made him feel awfully bad. He stood, up careful to kick some leaves over the place, and pulled up his pants.

Before the house started burning, the rider said he had to warn people the Yankees was fast coming. But where was Mamadear? They didn't even have a home now. He knew it was all gone. He could still smell the fire. The curtains, the beds, the rooms, his toy soldiers.

Slowly, he buttoned his pants all the way up and sat down in the pine needles. But then his stomach hurt so much he couldn't get comfortable. Gran Susie would have sung him a song. They were nigger songs, but he liked them. She would sing about trying to make Heaven my home, and steal away to Jesus, and he would go to sleep.

Daniel was with him when they came, and they hid in the swampy part of the pine stand. "We gots to hide, Marse Caswell," he said. "Get us some food and hide. Worry bout your mama later."

They were headed toward the kitchen, all the time knowing the Yankees were coming down the road. They found two loaves of Gran Susie's light bread, and then they heard the Yankees coming into the house, coming right into the house, walking on Mamadear's rugs and breaking up her things.

Daniel said, "Don't you let out a peep now," and they opened the back door and ran for the stand of pine trees near the house with the bread under their shirts, Daniel limping as fast as a jackrabbit. Daniel said he got his lame foot from a bad overseer in Virginia. "We'll wait till they gets what they wants, Marse Caswell, and then we'll go back to the house," he said. "They wants money, silver and food to fill their bellies. We gots to hide now."

So they waited a long time, and then Daniel left him to see was the coast clear, and he didn't come back. Caswell smelled fire and heard screaming and saw the firelight in the sky, and he knew Daniel was dead, and he knew the Yankee soldiers had done it. He didn't dare go to the house and see it burning.

There was nothing he could do to stop them. He didn't have a knife, so he just ran toward the river road.

He would get to the Burwell place as soon as it was light. He would find his Mamadear, and he knew she would know he had tried, but everybody had left him. He had to go to sleep now. Somehow, he had to go to sleep. If he could just find a good place.

He looked straight ahead. A little past the pine trees the ground dipped a little and there was a pine grove. He didn't know this place at all. There were frightening signs of rain, the rumbling of thunder and lightning streaks in the sky.

Caswell stumbled down an incline and stretched out at a place where the trees made a kind of shelter from the rain. It was starting to sprinkle, but it was less wet under there.

Then it started to rain harder and he had to try not to get too wet. He rested his head on his folded arms and curled up. He wouldn't think about snakes, and he would find his Mamadear as soon as he woke up.

CHAPTER 5

RABBIT

Daylily stirred a little, still exhausted in her sleep, and whimpered softly. Then her deep sleep was gradually broken by rustling—quiet at first, and then louder. She was all the way awake in seconds, her heart pounding. It was the soldiers coming back to get her; she knew it was.

She lay as still as she could, but her heart shook her whole body. The rustling turned into footsteps, and she heard somebody say, "What y'all doing here?" Her blood stopped. Didn't sound like a soldier; didn't sound like a White man.

Luke walked around to face her. "Hey, y'all sleeping?"

Daylily looked at the ground between her knees. At first she didn't move, but when she looked up and saw the tall, thin boy, she started to cry. Still, she was very glad it was a boy who had brown skin like her own and not a man. His eyes were big and bright.

"What you cryin bout, gal?" he said softly. Luke sat down next to her. He was tired and he was so hungry, his stomach was trying to touch his backbone.

"Who's this White chile here?"

Caswell was asleep about twelve feet away. "Don know,"

she said in a whisper. She was thinking about Buttercup and her babies just on the other side of the honeysuckle bushes where she had been hiding before she got up to get her drink. She didn't care about no White chile and how he come to be in the woods. She wiped her eyes and nose with her hands.

"Got to go home," she said. "Got to go. Granny be lookin for me." She tried to get up but fell back, dizzy. And then she remembered. Granny was dead. And more tears welled up in her eyes.

"Hey, gal, I said what you cryin bout, and what you doing here in these woods? You done cut out?" Luke shook her softly by the shoulders.

She knocked his hands off. Her shoulders stiffened. "Don't touch me," she said through her tears. "You ain't never seen me before. You don't even know my name."

"OK, OK," Luke said. He wished he had a rag to give her to wipe her face. "Look," he said after some silence, "I from the Higsaw place. Where you from?"

Daylily looked into the trees. Maybe he could help her get home. But maybe nobody was at home. She didn't know what she was going to do. She almost wished they had killed her like they killed them babies, then she wouldn't be here in these woods with this boy and that sleeping White chile. She couldn't keep her face dry, and she tried to use her shirt for a handkerchief and buried her face in her knees. "I b'long Massa Riverson," she told him softly.

"What you doing here then?" said Luke. "You done cut out?"

"Yankees done come, folks clear out, and Granny dead," she answered all at once. "Granny took sick, died, lef me with

Buttercup, and Yankee soldiers done killed her and her babies and here I be."

"Whew," Luke whistled. "Lawd-a mercy." It sounded terrible, but mostly it was confusing. He couldn't think of anything else to say except, "What you doing here with this White chile? And who you say got killed?"

"Buttercup and her babies. Got killed right over there not too far behind that honeysuckle. *He* ain't been here when all that done happened. I don't know how he come to be here," she said. "Reckon we should wake him up?"

They both turned toward Caswell, who was sleeping like a baby full of milk. Caswell's cheeks had reddened where his face was pressing against his arm.

"He wake up soon enough. Sun be shining on him and it's gonna be a hot day. It's past noon directly. You ain't got nobody now?" Luke asked her.

Daylily shook her head and looked past him at the trees. She couldn't get the words out. "You?" she said.

"Naw," said Luke. "Eugenia back at the kitchen. She the onliest family I got. I be lookin for some mens from the Higsaw place. Spose to meet them to join up with the Union, only I reckon the rain done scared em off. I'll find em. Sure, I'll find em soon enough." He could see the sun breaking through the trees and his stomach growled.

Caswell was finally awake. He sat up, his light brown hair was all messed up, and he thought he was dreaming, and then he remembered his mama. He had to find her and it was already late in the day. His clothes were full of brown mud. Then he saw the other two. His eyes were wide as a fawn's.

"Hey, chile," said Luke.

"My name's Caswell," he said. "Master Caswell to you."

"I ain't your nigger, Caswell," Luke reported, "and I ain't got to call you nothin I don't want to. Yankees done changed all that, Caswell."

"Smart-mouth niggers get whipped, boy." Caswell stood up, squaring his shoulders. "And I said my name is Master Caswell to you." His babyish voice sounded thin and scared.

"Ain't you the big man," Luke said, grinning at him. "And what you gon whup me with? I don't see nothin but your muddy drawers and your snotty nose or is I wrong? Is you got a whup hid somewhere behind you?" Luke ran around Caswell in circles. "Is you got it here, or here?"

Caswell turned around and around, trying to find a place to stand his ground. "My daddy will kill you soon's he come back from the war. He'll kill you just like he's killing them Yankees," he shouted.

Luke now knew that Caswell was probably alone and unprotected. "So your daddy's fighting the Yankees? Do tell! Then what you doing here? Why ain't you helping your daddy, you such a big man?" Luke had almost backed Caswell into a large tree trunk. "Why ain't you with your mama?"

"You can't make me answer," Caswell said. "None of your business. I've got to go. Get out of my way, nigger."

"How about you call me Luke, and then I move outta your way? You know, 'Luke' like they teach you in the White man's church? Luke and John and them other mens?"

Caswell tried ducking under Luke's arm. Luke grabbed him like a jackrabbit and held on to his shirt.

"You ain't called me Luke yet," he said, holding on to Caswell's arm.

"What we gonna do with him?" Luke said to Daylily.

"What you mean?"

"I mean what we gonna do? We can't let him go back where he come from; they be sending the dogs on us, saying we took him. You know how these rich White folks is. Besides, I run off, and I ain't taking no chances on being caught and being punished."

"They ain't sending no dogs on me," Daylily said. "I ain't run off. Marse Riverson say we be free to go. Folks just started running every which-a-way, and the last thing I know, we in the wagon leaving."

"Don't sound like you can go back," Luke said. "Anyway we got to keep him."

"You keep him," she said. "I don't want no parts of him."

"You ain't going nowhere, Caswell. You got to go with us. We's all going together. You get that through your little White head." He looked at Caswell's eyes, which were now filling up with tears.

I won't cry, Caswell thought. And then he said it out loud. "I won't cry. And I won't be kept by a nigger boy." He looked at Daylily as if she might help him, but she sat still, curious but silent.

Luke half dragged Caswell over to where Daylily sat. "See this rifle, boy? This mine. I took it from Massa Higsaw, and I do know how to shoot it, cause Unc Steph, he taught me to kill rabbits. And rifles kills peoples just as easy as they does rabbits. So you just set right here, rest your little behind right here, cause you ain't movin till us decides what to do with you."

Luke sat facing Daylily and Caswell, the gun across his knees. They were all quiet for a minute or two. Daylily was afraid to move; Caswell's big tears wet his chin.

"Well," said Luke, putting both his hands on his knees with all the authority he could muster, "look like I got to decide somethin."

They sat in silence for another full minute, Caswell sniffing up his tears and Daylily peering at Luke through eyes swollen with crying.

Finally Daylily couldn't stand it any more. "Stupid boy, you don't even know what to decide, do you? You don't know nothin. Bet you as scared as us is!"

Luke picked up his gun and dug the butt of it into the soil. "Awright! Awright!" he said. "This what us gon do. Us got to eat. Else we starve out here."

"See," said Daylily. "You so smart, what we gon eat? Grass? Ha! Grass!"

"Naw, you just like a gal. Don wait for nobody to finish. We gon eat rabbit and some squirrel and maybe some fish. You think you smart enough to catch us a fish?"

"Course I can," Daylily said. "I'm nine years old. I been knowing how to fish."

Caswell started, "My daddy said . . ."

"Hush up! Don't nobody wanna know what your daddy say," said Luke. "You just hush before I shoot your ear off. I gotta think." He thought very seriously. "Now, this what us gonna do. This gal here, what your name, gal?"

She looked at Luke like he was the devil's grandson. "Daylily," she said with her teeth closed.

"Daylily," Luke said, "you in charge of Caswell here." He grinned in triumph at the little boy. "Hold on to his trousers." Luke picked up a big rock off the ground. "Now, he get outta line, you whomp him upside his head with this here rock."

He was right, Daylily thought. They'd set the dogs on

them and she'd be caught. They wouldn't care about Butter-cup. They'd take Luke back to the Higsaw place, and maybe she'd be left alone again, and maybe those soldiers would come back and maybe not, but she didn't want to be alone again in these woods ever.

"Don't you move," she said to Caswell. Daylily hated Luke right then. She hated his orders, and she hated that he was right. She hated that he wasn't as scared as she was, at least he didn't act it. And she hated that she had to do what he said, or she'd be in the woods with no way out and no food. "Wait a minute," she said. "What you say your name was, boy?"

"Luke," he said over his shoulder. "Like in the Bible! I'm gon find us some food. Watch that White chile!"

When he walked off, there was an uncomfortable silence, and suddenly her fear grabbed at her again. She wished he'd come back even if she did hate him. She glanced at Caswell, gripping his wrist with one hand and the rock with the other. "Don't you move," she said, "or I'll hit you upside your head with this rock." She tried to look her meanest. He did look like he was afraid of her.

And so they sat for a half hour. Buzzards circled overhead. Daylily knew why, but she couldn't bear to think about it. She just wanted Luke to hurry up.

It was hot. Quiet in the woods. Gnats and mosquitoes bothered them. "I have to relieve myself," Caswell said.

"No, you ain't moving," Daylily said. "Not till Luke come back."

"But I have to go now," he whined. They sat another five minutes. Caswell began to wiggle.

"OK then," she said. "We'll walk over to them trees." They got up as if bonded together, the two of them and the rock. Daylily marched him over to the trees. Caswell stood there wiggling and waiting. "Do it then!" she ordered.

"Turn around," he said. "I ain't letting no nigger gal see me. Only Gran Susie can do that."

She turned away, still gripping his wrist and her rock. She could hear him trying to get his pants unbuttoned with his left hand.

"Wait," he said. "Can't get em down."

They switched hands. "Hurry up." She heard the water hit the leaves. "Hurry up!" she said again, feeling like she ought to help him; he was like the little ones she helped Granny with. But she had to make sure he knew she was the boss.

They made it back to where they had been sitting and plopped down. Daylily had to go too, but she wasn't about to do it while some stray White child watched her.

Ten minutes later they heard a loud shot.

"Whooee," Luke hollered. "Got em!" In a minute he was there holding a rabbit by the feet. "Lookee what I got," he said, grinning from one side of his face to the other. "First shot! Dinner." He took Aunt Eugenia's knife out of his overalls pocket. "Now we got to skin it and start up a fire. Oh man, rabbit meat!"

Daylily said, "Who gon watch him?" She pointed at Caswell. "I got to go do somethin."

Luke looked away from her face. He pointed his gun at Caswell. "Go on. I got him covered," he said, glaring at the little boy.

Daylily scrambled up. Her bottom hurt from the long wait, but she flew into the woods, trying to get away from them so they wouldn't hear her pee trickling down on the leaves.

Then she got a long drink from the river, careful not to go anywhere she knew she'd find the dead bodies.

She washed her face and hands, and scrubbed her cinnamon skin, and tried to braid her hair. It was matted with mud. She'd have to wash it in the river later.

"Where you been, gal?" Luke said when she returned. "I got to skin this rabbit so we can eat. Here, hold this rifle on this boy. Can you shoot? You sho look a heap better."

"Course I can," she said, even though she had never held a rifle before. "You ain't too clean yourself, you know."

He ignored her remark. "Well, watch him, cause we gon eat in a little while," he said, beginning to work on the rabbit.

Luke slit and skinned the rabbit just like Unc Steph had taught him. He put it on a stick, and piled up his firewood. He took out Massa Higsaw's flint and steel to strike a spark.

"Tomorrow us gon have fish?" Luke said, looking at Daylily with a sly grin. He didn't believe she knew how to fish at all.

She hadn't thought about tomorrow. Was there a tomorrow? Would they ever see anybody else, or would they just be in the woods forever? And where was everybody she knew? Where was little Bubba, and Marylynn, and Andrew, and all the rest of them? Were they all dead like Granny and Buttercup and her babies?

Caswell sat a few feet from Daylily and thought about his Mamadear having dinner at the Burwell plantation. Tomorrow he'd find a way to escape, as soon as he had some rabbit to eat.

The rabbit looked a nice brown color as Luke turned it around and around on the stick. "Y'all better come on," he said finally. "It sure is ready now!" His eyes sparkled even more as Daylily started to get up.

"Wait, we got to do this right," Luke said. "I'll eat first cause I shot that rabbit, and then I'll watch him and you eat," he said to Daylily. "And he'll eat last cause we in charge a him."

In Aunt Eugenia's kitchen Luke could never eat till all the White folks had seconds, then thirds, and then all the food was cleared from the table. He tore off a large piece of meat while Daylily and Caswell looked on. "Y'all just don't know," he blurted out with a full mouth, "how good that was!" He shook his head from side to side and wiped his mouth with his sleeve. "Think I'll have me another little piece," he said, pretending to reach for the rest of the meat.

Daylily turned toward him with the gun in her hand, and Luke fell back laughing with delight. She grabbed her share and pushed the gun at him.

"Here, you watch him, you crazy boy," she said, tearing into the rabbit.

"Man, you sho is hungry," he said. "You is sho serious about that rabbit!"

After his meal, Caswell demanded a drink from the river, and they all flopped down next to the river, watching the leaves and the clouds drifting up above. It was quiet until Luke said, "I smell something funny."

Daylily had smelled it too.

"Where you say your friend, you know, Butter . . ."

"They's over there," she said in a whisper. Luke turned and looked where she had pointed.

"They's over there," she said again in a whisper. The good rabbit rose in her throat.

Luke's mouth opened as if to say something. He blinked. "Naw," he said. "Naw, it ain't *this* close, is it?"

She nodded furiously.

"Les move then," he said, gathering up his knife and rifle and stamping out the fire. The afternoon was on its way. "Les move out. We got to go. Somebody else sure to smell em soon. Soldiers thinking they's needing to bury the dead. That smell be strong and then somebody find us. We got to walk away from here as fast as we can."

He felt his mam's mojo around his neck. Folks that was murdered and dead before their time didn't rest easy. He knew that.

"I ain't goin," Caswell said all of a sudden. He hadn't spoken in an hour.

"You *is* goin," said Luke. "You don't, I'll go upside yo skinny head! Get over here."

"I ain't. I'm goin to run away to the Burwell place. That's where my Mamadear is and you can't stop me!"

Luke grabbed him by the arm, and the younger boy struggled to get free, but he was too small to give Luke much of a problem.

"Now you march, you," Luke said, "cause I ain't gonna end up like them three over there on the ground, and Daylily neither."

Caswell was suddenly attentive. "What three?" he said, standing still.

"Them three dead people, that's what. Didn't you hear that gal talkin bout Yankee soldiers killing Buttercup and her babies? Well, you run away like you want to, only you be sure you run in that direction toward them honeysuckle bushes."

Luke stuck out his arm in the direction none of them wanted to go. "You run right over there and look behind them bushes at them bodies and see does you want to be in these woods by yourself. Dead peoples be in these woods, that's what, and Yankees done killed them. You still want to be goin to the Burwell plantation by yourself?"

Caswell was speechless with fear. Dead people were worse than live Yankees and niggers put together, so he gave in, and they marched on along the riverbank, Luke trying to put as much distance between himself and the dead as possible, Day-lily thinking how she didn't want to think about buzzards, and Caswell howling into the failing afternoon sun.

CHAPTER 6

TREASURE

It was early September and so the heat was fickle, some nights warm and some bringing a slight chill. Last night's rain had broken the heat, at least for now. They walked in silence once Caswell was tired of crying and Luke was tired of yelling at him to shut up. Up hill and down. It would be sunset soon. Luke started looking for a place to sleep.

Straight ahead the river road split. In the distance was what looked like an abandoned shed, but Luke didn't want to risk being found, and the road looked like it was curving away from the river. The river made a slight turn here and got much wider.

Daylily was gazing over toward the left. Luke thought she was watching the sunset. A gray haze spread out over part of the sky.

"Smells like smoke," she said. For a moment, she was silent. Then she said, "We should go this way," and pointed opposite the orange and lavender sky so beautiful and distant.

Luke turned toward the shack, more than a little apprehensive but too tired to think what else to do. He was starting to feel responsible for the younger children. Caswell lagged behind, taking smaller and smaller steps. Finally, Daylily went back and took him by the hand. Luke felt his powder bag. "Wait," he said, as he got closer and closer to the shelter. "Lemme see is it safe."

It was a small place, but he could tell it was the back of an old farmhouse. There were fields going to seed; a half-burned house in the distant twilight shadows, its chimneys poking up into the purple sky; a plow and wagon left behind. All he could hear were a few crickets and mosquitoes buzzing. "Must have been terrible," he muttered to himself, and then waved his hand to the others to come ahead.

A hawk flew overhead into the black trees. There was no door on the shed, but it would give them somewhere to be out of the cool at night. They saw that someone else had been there. An old wool jacket and a rusty knife and fork were on the floor.

Caswell curled up on the raggedy jacket and was asleep in a few minutes.

Daylily leaned her back against the wall of the tiny place. "He ain't gon find his mama," she whispered to Luke, who had collapsed beside her.

"Who care?" Luke moaned. "You think maybe we should let him go try?"

"No, I mean, he ain't," she repeated. She leaned over very close to Luke's ear. "Burwell place be burned down. I saw it from the river road. Ain't no Burwell place no more."

"You mean you knowed that all along?" Luke said.

"No, I saw it from the road up there just now when I said we should go this way. I know where Burwells' is. I been there once. Us went to help Missus dress at a big party and spend the night. All I see tonight is smoke. He just too little to see over them trees and bushes, and he don't know where he is nohow. So we stuck with him. He ain't got nowhere to go and maybe his mammy dead too."

Luke shook his head and put his arms across his forehead. He was worn out. Still, he couldn't get to sleep right away. He thought this must have been the longest day in his life. Being in the woods with this strange girl and this little White boy. All kind of pictures in his head. Daylily say her granny died, say she belong to Massa Riverson. Something about a woman who was killed in the woods with her two babies by some Yankee soldiers, and she left alone, and then they find this White chile sleeping under a tree who was hollering about finding his Mamadear and his daddy killing Yankees and maybe killing them too.

And only God knew where this White boy's Mamadear was at. Yankee soldiers could-a killed her too. It was a whole lot to think on, a terrible lot to think on. Then there was Aunt Eugenia. She would be worried sick by now, wondering where he was, and he out in this woods, which was far as he got looking for Unc Steph. He wanted to find the Union soldiers.

Maybe Daylily was wrong and them soldiers who killed that woman and her babies wasn't Yankee. Girls didn't know nothing. He knew he could fight, even if he was just a boy. Somebody needed to fight. Folks losing they families and all. He knew about that.

Luke felt his eyes tearing up under his arm. He didn't want to cry, but nobody could see him in the dark. He sniffed up the tears and remembered that Unc Steph said when things get too bad, go to sleep. Always look better in the morning time. Maybe that's why the good Lord made sleep.

• • •

Morning came, but it came noisy and frightening. It came with sounds of guns and battle in their ears. They heard it almost all at once.

"Lord-a mercy what is it?" Daylily gasped, sitting straight up, her eyes wide open as they could get.

"Guns," said Luke. "Hush, they's mighty near."

Caswell almost got through the door before Daylily grabbed the seat of his pants.

"Don't you know nothin, boy? You get yourself killed!" she said.

In the midst of the noise, Caswell yelled something about runnin off and killin Yankees and findin his daddy, and they pulled him down and held him still.

"Now you look-a here," Luke said fiercely. "You run out there and you gets killed. They'll shoot you cause you so little they won't see you and then they come lookin and they finds us. And another thing . . ." Daylily shot Luke a look and shook her head.

"Just be quiet," he told the boy, understanding her. "We got to stay here and pray to the Lord they don't find us."

Caswell glared at Luke but sat still. The noise went on all day, it seemed. Screams of victory and agony all mixed together. It was happening over in the next gully, but it was so loud they sometimes had to hold their ears. All they could see from the doorway was a cloud of smoke, and then the whole thing stopped, it seemed, as suddenly as it had started. There was the uneasy quiet that comes after a fury has been let loose.

In the deep silence, the three of them didn't speak.

Finally, Daylily sighed. "What us gon do? Us can't sit here forever."

Still they waited, all of them afraid to move. The shock of the noise, the fear and the silence had them hypnotized.

"Us got to eat sometime today. You reckon it safe to move?" she whispered.

Luke said nothing. He was concentrating on what he knew he had to do. Guns meant fighting and danger, and he sure wished he didn't have to go out there.

"I seen blackberries over there, Luke," she said, trying again.

"Can't get no berries till I check," Luke said. "Watch him. I got to see can we move from here."

He was scared. Anybody'd be scared to go out there. And what if somebody grabbed him? The younger ones looked at Luke as if he should know what to do. Daylily held on to Caswell's hand, and he didn't even struggle this time.

Luke ran his hand over his face. If only Unc Steph was with him now. He sighed twice and pulled on his pants as if to jack them up. "Don't y'all move," he said. "I'll be right back," and he stepped out into the afternoon sunlight quietly.

Luke moved straight ahead, looking from side to side as he padded up a small hill. The afternoon sun shone on every blade of grass. Goldenrod blew softly in the breeze.

But what he saw on the other side of the hill made him close his eyes and clap his hands over them. He just stood there in the grass, a young boy growing old second by second. He saw it all at once. It was like a dream, and he knew he'd never forget it. Before him was a field, a harvest of death, a sea of arms and legs, cotton and wool and metal, dead horses, and everywhere black and red stains spreading their fingers, spreading over what once were heads, hands, and private parts.

Luke fell back as if pushed by a force he couldn't see. When he came to himself, he was retching on what little was in his stomach, his nut-brown face a gray cast. He sat very still. So this was what he had left home for. This was war. Unc Steph and the others, they could be out there. What did God mean, letting such things happen? He had run away from the master for this?

He slammed his fist into the ground, and it was only his hand that felt it, not the hard-packed dirt, or even the butterfly that had found its way to a pink clover blossom next to him and fluttered off. Luke slammed his fist again and again, until he had made a dent in the earth. Tears covered his chin, and he choked on them. Then he remembered the others.

I can't let them see me crying like an old woman, he thought. If he didn't get back, they would be coming to find him before long. He couldn't let them see this, a girl, and a little White boy who was already spooked about his mama. They needed water too, he remembered, feeling his throat tighten.

He looked straight ahead into the field and suddenly began to get angry. He didn't like that this could happen and people could be there one day and gone the next. He thought about Aunt Eugenia and the others he cared about. They wouldn't want him to give up. If nobody but Daylily and Caswell knew he was alive, then they would have to be his friends. He was the oldest, he thought, swallowing hard, and he would just have to be the one who saved them. Luke stared at the mass of bodies. He remembered his mojo only when he grabbed his shirt to wipe his face and felt it.

His nostrils went rigid with determination. He inched his

way toward the hellhole in front of him, closer and closer to the bodies of soldiers, some not much older than him. He was looking for three coats, and canteens and some more gunpowder and pellets. He would have to touch them, pull off their coats and look in their pockets, look into their eyes.

He avoided bodies that had no arms and legs, turning his head, reaching out timidly and then snatching back his hands. The dead were already beginning to stink. He wanted to do it without looking at them, but there was no way to miss them, no place to walk without seeing.

Only one jacket came off easily. He would always remember the ragged limbs, the feel of the stiff bloodstains on the coat. The soldier's arms were pulled back, and his coat was unbuttoned. Luke cut the strap holding the powder sack and the canteen with his own knife. With one done, he felt a kind of triumph over this awful work. He could do what he was doing and not die himself. After that their faces became just a blur of flesh.

Finally, he had taken more than he could carry. Three coats, canteens, a pocket New Testament, gunpowder, hats, knives and even a few letters and coins, two pairs of shoes and most wonderful of all, a bayonet. He had to drop some things at the top of the hill and make two trips.

There was no way to tell what color some of the uniforms had been or how many of each. A few of the men had worn farm shirts and overalls. If the rebs won, he reasoned, it'd be dangerous to stick around. If it was Union soldiers who won, would they keep him or kill him?

He knew some Black folks followed the soldiers for food. So much had shaken his confidence. The world had turned itself around on him, and he was no longer sure how anything would work. Better to keep on the run and be far away from this battleground before he trusted anybody.

He found Daylily and Caswell asleep from exhaustion. They had given out from hunger and the fear of not knowing what had happened to him. The sun was low in the sky.

Luke decided to surprise them with blackberries. He took the three Confederate hats he had found, and filled them with blackberries to present with his other gifts.

When he got back to the shed, the others were still asleep. Luke tried to stay awake to make sure Caswell didn't sneak off. Finally, he put his head down on his folded arms. Maybe he should just go on home. He thought about his mam again. Whenever he'd ask Aunt Eugenia why they killed his mam, she'd say because she was too much trouble.

Aunt Eugenia would wipe her eyes quick on her apron and say something about onions making her eyes water, so he wouldn't know she was crying, but he knew.

She'd say, "She was just sick at heart was all. Your mama was just sick at heart," and then she'd say, "Go long now, don't ask me no more."

Maybe his mam could see him up in Heaven. He could feel himself getting sleepy and he was glad. He was tired of thinking of Aunt Eugenia, Unc Steph, the dead men blown apart, all of it, over and over. As he drifted off, pictures of his mam's face floated through his mind. Her name was Lucymae. He missed her.

When she woke up from her nap, Luke was sitting there chewing.

"Ooh, what are you eating?" Daylily asked. "You got berries. I can see your mouth all blue round your lips. You got berries. Gimme some!"

Luke shook his head. "Nope. They mine."

Daylily protested. "That ain't fair!"

By this time Caswell was awake. "I want some," he whined. "I should have some too."

"You don't even know what I got," Luke said. He was hiding the berries under the coat he'd just found a few hours before. He uncovered the rest of the berries with a flourish. "There! I brought y'all a surprise! We got berries for supper!"

Daylily looked at the berries in the hats. "Where you get these hats, Luke?"

"Found em, on the ground. Eat them berries and say thank you."

She was already licking the juice off her lips.

CHAPTER 7

GOOD-BYE

The berries were good, but by morning her stomach felt empty again. She hated to think of the sun coming up because she had to tell Caswell. Otherwise he'd be yelling about his Mamadear forever. They had spent another night in the shed, because Luke said they needed to wait until morning to start out again. Besides he heard voices of men over on that battle-field and he knew that they were probably soldiers burying the dead. They were all hungry, but looking for food meant going out there where there were dangerous men and dead bodies.

Daylily was lying wrapped in her coat. A bad smell hit her nostrils as soon as she was fully awake. It was still dark. They were all sleeping warm for the first time in two nights. She took a sip of water from her canteen and Caswell sat up slowly. He looked terrible. His eyes were red rimmed. He had been crying for two days and had thrown up yesterday.

"I got to go," he said to Daylily. She glanced in Luke's direc-tion. He was sleeping hard. There was no sense waking Luke yet, but she knew Caswell was going to raise a ruckus. She put her finger across her lips, indicating he should be quiet, and took him outside the shack, checking first one direction and then the other.

They seemed to be entirely alone. The sky was a soft gray, just before sunrise. Daylily looked quickly toward what she knew had been the Burwell place. Still, she took him behind a scrubby bush near the shed.

"I got to tell you somethin," she said softly as he unbuttoned his pants. In the two days they'd been on the road, he'd given up hiding himself from her, and watched her face as he peed. He always had trouble closing his pants back up. Daylily thought he couldn't have been more than six or maybe seven. The boy was probably used to some mammy doing that for him. She finished the trouser buttons and put her hands around his waist and sat him down on the ground. "I got to tell you bout your mama."

"You don't know nothin about my mama," Caswell said. He picked at a bug bite of some kind. "You jus a nigger gal. How could you know something about my Mamadear? She's a lady."

"I knows where the Burwell place was," Daylily insisted, and she hurried on now, wanting to get it over with. "And it's all gone. It's burned down, Caswell. It's gone."

He spit out his lower lip, which was beginning to tremble in spite of the scorn he tried to show. "How do you know that?"

"Because I been there. I been there with my granny. It's not a far piece from here. We was almost there day before yesterday when we saw this shed and I smelled the smoke. You can see the place from here. Used to be on a hill, and you can see it all gone. You was too sleepy last night for me to tell you."

He was up and running into the gloom of the early dawn

before she had the words out. Suddenly, he disappeared in the tall grass. She darted after him; as he fell, she caught him by the pants. His elbow was bleeding a little.

"Show me," he wailed. "Show me. I don't believe you!"

Daylily knew that he would never be quiet until she did, so she stood him up, and together they walked to the fork in the road. They went close enough to see in the distance a strange blackened hole with great chimneys and what had been a grand entranceway that now led to nowhere. Early morning mist floated about in the ruins. It stank of smoke and fire. "That was it, Caswell. That was where you was headed."

He just stood there as if nailed to the ground. And then he clutched himself around the waist and began to rock back and forth. He rocked and wailed, "Nononono." The only witnesses besides Daylily were satiny blackbirds who began to caw, and the mockingbird who answered Caswell with its beautiful morning song.

Daylily held on to him. She gave him what nobody had given her, rocking him like a baby, but moaning for herself. Their cries rose over the field ruined with blood and ash, and up into the dawn pink with the sun's fire.

CHAPTER 8

FISHING FOR DINNER

Luke woke with a start and looked around for the others. They were not there. His heart began to beat faster. He was sweating and trembling some, and he had dreamed of being buried alive by soldiers who had no hands or faces. Today, there'd be more soldiers here; he knew that. It would take more than one day to bury all those men. He scrambled up, yearning for a biscuit, and then that awful death smell took his yearning away and he took a swallow of water from a canteen instead.

They had to hurry. It was dangerous to stay here any longer. He knew the soldiers were out there.

A few minutes later he found Caswell and Daylily outside sitting together in silence, their faces streaked with dirt and tears. Luke looked like a traveling junk man. He had put on one of the coats and brought along everything else, the bayonet and rifle under his right arm, two coats under his left, one pair of shoes on his feet and one under the coats. Three canteens were draped around his neck, clanking as he walked, and his pockets were full of gunpowder and pellets. There were three hats on his head, and his curly hair stuck out all around the caps. In the distance he could hear the sergeant giving orders to the burial detail.

Daylily looked up at him as he approached. "I done tole him," she said. "I done tole him his mama gone, and he done pitched a fit worse'n a mad dog."

"We ain't got time now, we got to go," Luke said, shifting all his burdens. "Here, put on these coats."

"What's stinkin' so bad? Smells like more dead folks," said Daylily.

"They be just over that hill burying dead folks," Luke answered. "Here, you all. Put on these coats. We got to go."

Instead of taking the coat Daylily only stared at it.

Luke looked at her with a steady gaze. His jaw was set. He didn't flinch. For a minute he thought of telling Daylily that her coat had been on a dead man, and scaring her half to death with all the pictures that were in his head of blown-off hands and exploded stomachs and worse. But he couldn't. He knew that two days ago he would have done it just to hear her holler, to see her throw her coat on the ground and run, and he knew she'd have said something like, "Boy, take this ugly thing away from here. It be cursed or something!"

But something had happened that made him different. He didn't know what it was, but he couldn't bring himself to tease her that way. A part of him was gone, and some other part was there instead. Part of him wanted to understand why men would fight and die like pigs being slaughtered, and part of him wanted to prove that he wasn't afraid of what he had seen any more. For the first time he really knew he had blood in his body that could spill out in the dirt, and nobody might not even see it, or even care, not the way he cared when they beat his Mam to death. How could people just kill you and leave you in the dirt to rot? He wanted to understand that.

So he wasn't the same. He couldn't make fun of Daylily like he always did the girls back on the place, and he couldn't tease Caswell about his Mamadear, who was most likely dead in the fire. He ought to say something about Daylily's granny and Caswell's Mamadear, but he didn't know what the words would be, even if he tried, so all he said was "You right. Them's dead men you smell."

Daylily opened her mouth, as if she had been told to take something that would make her sick.

"We ain't got time to talk now. We got to go," Luke said, "fore they comes this way. We got to get back to the river road and get into the woods so's they don't find us." His canteens banged together while he struggled with the coats, and the shoes fell into the dust. He dropped the three hats trying to hold on to his rifle.

Daylily started to giggle. She picked up the hats. It seemed a relief for her to laugh at something. She grinned and showed her two dimples. "You sure is a sight," she said. "You is a sight with all them geehaws on you!"

Even Caswell had started to smile. He was fascinated by the canteens and kept touching the bayonet Luke had found. Finally he tried to take it out of Luke's hand.

Luke shook Caswell off and glared at the two of them. "Just you take these coats and hurry up about it. This ain't no time for lollygaggin now." They scrambled into their coats, and he hung a canteen around each of their necks, tying the straps together that he had cut off the dead soldiers. "Here, these your shoes," he said to Daylily.

She looked at him and wrinkled up her mouth.

"How I'm gon wear these? They way too big."

"Just keep em," he ordered. "You never know how far we is got to walk. Caswell's feet be fine. He got them good White folks' shoes on. Sides, his feet be way too small. Les go. Hurry up."

"I want to carry the sword," Caswell said, eyeing the bayonet.

Daylily carried her contraband shoes by the laces, and everybody had a hat on.

"Naw, you way too little," Luke said. "Anyway, it ain't no real sword. It just part of a sword broken off a gun. It be too heavy for you, and sides, you might stab me and run away."

Caswell's eyes began to fill up. He took Daylily's hand. "I want to carry the sword," he said again. And then slowly, "Please, Luke."

Luke gave in. "Oh, come on then, les go!" He handed Caswell the bayonet.

Caswell held the bayonet as if he had his very own precious treasure.

Luke was nervous. "They getting closer. Us got to hustle! And be quiet too. Don't you think I ain't watching you, Caswell."

Caswell looked straight ahead and turned away from the Burwell place as they passed it. His soldier's coat dragged the ground. Luke was as tense as a deer, watching and listening for Confederate soldiers. They made a little battalion of their own, moving north into the trees, the sun coming up full in the east.

• • •

They had been walking for an hour with their own thoughts. Nobody had had much to say.

Finally Daylily broke the silence with a sneeze. "Lordy, ah'm hungry," she sighed.

Luke stopped walking. "We need us a fish line," he said to her. He looked in all their pockets for string they could tie to a pole. In one of the pockets there was something that looked like a wire.

"Catgut," Daylily said. "That's what they use to string a banjo. That soldier must have played the banjo and stuffed the extra strings in the pocket of his jacket." She searched for the right tree branch to use for a pole and tied the catgut strings together to make one long string.

She felt more peaceful today, like it didn't much matter what happened to them now. Digging in the mud with Luke's knife, she thought about Granny's kitchen garden, and the greens she used to be so proud of.

Luke and Caswell just watched her. They both sat down on the banks of the river. Luke brushed aside some twigs and got comfortable.

"You know what you doin, gal?" he said.

"It good night crawlers in here." She ignored his put-down. "Us got to find a hook, y'all." She moved a few feet away, looking for a good place to throw in the line.

"You find it, I'm plum wore out," Luke answered.

"I'll be mighty glad to eat all my fish myself," she said, busy with her pole and her worms. She took the knife and made a groove on the pole so the string wouldn't slip off.

Luke looked in his pocket.

"Ain't no hooks gonna be in this pocket," said Luke. He shook his head, as if to say she was on a fool's errand. Then he saw the medal pinned to his coat. "Look like we in luck," he called to her. "Come get this pin."

"If you can't get up," she shouted, "I'm eatin this fish myself. Me and Caswell. Caswell, bring me the hook."

Caswell was gazing into the water, a million miles into the past.

"Wait now, wait. I got to fix it for you," said Luke, all business all of a sudden. "Girl, you don't even know what to do with this here pin." He broke off the hook on the back of the medal and put it back in his pocket. "Here, now, mind you don't lose it, you know how you gals is."

Daylily looked at the little pin from the medal and then at him. "You got to bend it, boy," she said. "You don't have no sense sometimes. You got to bend it for the crawler and the string." She handed it back to him.

Luke worked with the hook until he had it shaped for a worm. "Mind you put that hook on the string good," he said. "It's the onliest one we got. Some big ole fish swallow it and it be gone."

"You just make a fire," she said, stretching out her brown legs and leaning against a tree, "and leave me be to catch us some dinner."

Daylily's fishing was a triumph and a lifesaver. She put the hook and line very carefully into her pocket. Their stomachs filled again, with a fish left over, Luke wrapped the little cooked sunfish in his handkerchief and they kept moving.

CHAPTER 9

MUNDA AND THE THREE-LEGGED DOG

It was now their fifth day in the woods. The day before, Luke had shot a squirrel, but it made a thin meal for them.

Ever since he had learned about his Mamadear, Caswell's eyes followed Daylily everywhere. When she washed her hands in the river, he'd wait, nervous until she came back. When she disappeared behind the trees for privacy, he'd wait impatiently until she reappeared.

He constantly followed her with his eyes, except when they were around the fire at night. Then he watched the flames with wide-open eyes that had great circles under them that made his face look as pale as a winter sky.

Luke was holding a rabbit between his knees that he had just shot for their supper.

Daylily watched Caswell watching the fire. She poked at Luke softly and motioned that he should look at Caswell too. It worried her, this thing that happened to him around the fire, and it worried her that he watched her all the time.

"He bout right in the head, you reckon?" she whispered to Luke. "You reckon he take it into his head to run?" They were sitting on part of a fallen pecan tree. Daylily was next to Luke and Luke was next to Caswell. They had stopped there be-cause they saw a few pecans on the ground, but it was too early in the season, and the nuts weren't good. They were still green.

"Naw, he all right." Luke seemed confident.

Still Daylily watched Caswell carefully and tried to talk to him. She had an idea, and she moved around Luke and sat next to Caswell on the end of the pecan log.

"I tell you what we could do," she said, putting her arm around him. "We could tell stories to pass the time. Would you like that?"

Caswell didn't answer, but she kept on talking anyway. "I know," she said brightly. "You can tell us about your home place. What was it like where you live?" Then Daylily gri-maced slightly, realizing that she had made a mistake. He would be remembering his Mamadear.

Caswell blinked and looked right at Daylily. "They killed Daniel!" he said. "They killed Daniel!"

His outburst startled Daylily. She shook him slightly. "Cas-well, don't fret yourself!" she said quickly, but he kept talking, and then he told them all about the fire that burned up his house and how he came to be in the woods. After that he seemed to want to hear them talk, and he wanted to hear about their lives back home.

Luke said, "I ain't telling him no stories."

But Daylily didn't mind. "Please, Luke, it keep him from starin like that," she said.

Luke peered at Caswell. "Y'all go head," he said, because it was starting to give him the creeps watching Caswell look at the fire like he was going to jump into it.

Kicking at the green pecans that were on the ground, Luke

sighed. "Y'all can start the stories. Ain't nobody gonna fix this rabbit I done caught for us, so I reckon I better get started. I'll tell mine after we eat."

Daylily shook her head. "I hope I don't never see another rabbit in my whole life, when us gets to wherever we goin," she said.

While Luke was skinning the rabbit, and Daylily was keeping the fire going, Caswell suddenly blurted out, "My Mamadear's name is Miss Loddy. What's your mama's name, Luke?"

Luke looked away from them into the trees. He sighed. "Was Lucymae. She dead."

"What's your mama's name, Daylily?" Caswell persisted.

"Granny," she said. "She raise me. She ain't my real mama though. Don't have no real mama, just have Granny."

"Granny what?" Caswell screwed up his forehead as if he was confused.

"Just Granny." Daylily was drawing a little design in the dust with a stick. She turned the corners of her mouth down. She was drawing a quilt pattern she was learning from Granny. The flying geese pattern. Granny said it was a secret code for slaves to get free.

She was going to make it with some scraps from Missus' old dresses. Now she guessed she'd never make it. She threw the stick down in the dust.

"What happened to your real mama?" Caswell said.

"She was sold from the place, I reckon, or dead. Don't know. Time to eat now, don't ask me no more."

After he nibbled a little bit of meat, Caswell lay on his side and closed his eyes. Daylily sure hoped he would go on to sleep. She looked at Caswell and noticed he had a large scar on his ear. For a minute, she wondered how he got that scar, but then she didn't think about it any more. She had her own worries.

Now it was her turn to look into the fire. She didn't like to think about home, about Granny and Buttercup and Mary-lyn and all the rest of them. It was too hard. And her chest hurt when she thought about it. The fire crackled and sang with the popping wood. Sparks flew out into the purple dark-ness. Daylily coughed. She felt kind of sick. Maybe she had the miseries comin, like Granny used to say. It would soon be night again, and she felt lower and lower.

"Ain't you got no stories you can tell, Luke?" Daylily said. She kept trying to braid her hair, but it wasn't much use with-out a comb. Luke sat over next to her.

"Well, maybe," he said. He didn't want to think much about home or about anybody he loved, but maybe he could tell something that was exciting and keep them from being so sad.

Luke and Daylily whispered along with the dogwood and pecan trees that were in this part of the woods. The cool was coming on with the night. Luke looked up at the night sky. He was searching for the drinking gourd, but he didn't see it.

Luke was now as worried as Daylily about Caswell staring into the fire. There was no telling what he'd do, and Luke didn't feel like fishing anybody out of the fire. And what if he burned himself? Then what would they do to help him? Back there after he saw the dead soldiers, Luke realized all they had was each other, so they all had to stay alive and they had to take care of each other.

Luke tried to get comfortable on the ground. It seemed as

hard as that anvil he had seen Elijah the blacksmith using to shoe horses. He didn't have much fat left to spare him the rocks and roots. "Lemme see," he said as he threw some pine-cones out of his way.

He could smell the pine needles and hear the crickets and squirrels scurrying around. He thought about that dog at the home place named Black Nigger. Massa Higsaw named him that, and every time he called out "Black Nigger" to the dog, somebody on the place would jump to see was he calling them. Then Massa Higsaw would laugh like it was the best joke he'd ever heard. He thought that was real funny. Luke shook his head. He used to laugh too. Now it didn't seem so funny.

"Come on, Luke, please," Daylily coaxed. "I can't sleep noway."

"All right, I'm just doing this so you leave me alone," Luke said. He turned over on his side and leaned on his elbow.

"Was a three-legged dog on the place," he said to Daylily. "Name Black Nigger. Dog took to some and hated some. Folks say Black Nigger was trained to kill if Massa Higsaw ordered him to. I never did know if this was true, but us knew he was meaner than the devil.

"Some say if he looked you straight in the eye, it meant you was gonna die soon, cause he was a devil dog. Us knew he just as soon take a bite out your leg as look at you, and the darker you was, the worse that dog hated you.

"He was trained by Massa Higsaw to hate Black. Saw him bite a man once. Was a terrible thing. Almost clean through his leg. Didn't let loose till Massa told him to let go. Folks say this man smart-mouthed Massa Higsaw.

"Unc Steph say that dog was sent from hell just to give

niggers trials and tribulation. Was a big ole ugly dog, you
know, slobbering and growling. I reckon I was more scared a
him than anything with two legs."

Daylily was wondering why she'd ever asked for a story,
but still it was better than crying about home, or thinking
about who or what was out there in those dark trees. She
wrapped her coat around her tightly and held her arms together, afraid to look anywhere but into the fire.

"Munda was a field hand on the place, Massa Higsaw had
a wager about Munda. Folks say Munda tried to get some of
his own back with Black Nigger. Folks say Munda died on
purpose and almost took Black Nigger along for the ride to
hell. Only Black Nigger didn't die. He come out the wager
with three legs and it messed up his huntin nose, so Massa lost
his prize dog and his prize nigger all at the same time."

Daylily shifted and lay down with her head propped up on
her arms.

"Unc Steph don tole me how it happened. One day, one
fine and fair day, Massa say he want to prove to his friends
that Munda could plow more fields in a single day than Massa
Johnstoner's prize nigger Tommy, so they had a wager, you
know?"

Daylily wasn't sure what a wager was. She shook her head.

"It's a way mens see who's best," said Luke with a slightly
superior tone. "They uses money and who wins, gets the
money. Massa Higsaw had lotsa wagers. He gambled with
cards mostly, so he owed Massa Johnstoner lots of money. So,
Massa Johnstoner wagered his Tommy gainst Munda. Said
he'd forgive the debt if Munda wins, and if Tommy win,
he'd take Munda instead of money. Cause Munda worth so
much money, Massa Higsaw real nervous about the wager,

but he also don't want to pay all that money back to Massa Johnstoner.

"He tell Munda he better win, or else he be sorry. Course that didn't scare Munda much cause if he lost, he be owned by Massa Johnstoner.

"He already strong as a mule and meaner than a rattlesnake being bit by a mad dog, but Munda, he wanna leave the place. He hate Massa Higsaw worse'n anything, and he figger Massa Johnstoner a better man and maybe he could buy out his free-dom, which he heard tell of folks doin over there. They say Massa Johnstoner was a fair man as White folks go. So Munda, he bound and determined to lose this here wager.

"Tommy was plowing that field like a man gone mad. Up one row and down the other. Up and down, pushing that mule, wearing one out and calling for another, and Munda was pushing up and down the other side of the field, but he was going slower than he could have, letting Tommy take the lead. Ole Munda was on his way to winning a better life by losing; that's what he thought.

"Now the thing is, he hate this other nigger Arkansas even worser than he hate Massa Higsaw, and don't nobody know why for sho, but Arkansas give Munda the evil eye every day in the field and Munda threaten to beat him up every night when dark come, and so they just spoiling for a fight some kinda way. Maybe over a woman, that's what Gustavus say.

"Unc Steph saw the whole thing. In the middle of plowing a row, Munda happened to look up and saw Arkansas out of the corner of his eye, taking pure advantage of the contest to cut and run. Way over in the distance, he was working his way through the trees, quiet-like, from tree to tree. Didn't nobody else notice cause all us cheering and watchin, and that included

Overseer Dugun, who wasn't too smart anyway, plus Massa
Higsaw, Massa Johnstoner and Black Nigger. All us watching
to see who would win the plowing. We ain't seen nobody was
missing and we sure ain't lookin into the trees.

"When Munda spy Arkansas, he just stop plowing, and
he look Black Nigger straight in the eye and holler, 'Black
Nigger! . . . Sic em, Nigger!' and he point to the woods.
Black Nigger let loose runnin like a wild animal, clamp his
teeth on Arkansas' leg and drag him out of the trees. He be
yelling and screaming, blood everywhere, and Munda, he saw
he done lost the contest cause Tommy just kept on plowin. He
wasn't lookin at no devil dog.

"Munda just standing there grinning, not even tryin to
win, just glad he lost the race and Arkansas got caught. Massa
got so mad that he bout to lose his best worker to Massa Johnstoner, and that Arkansas' leg was tore up, he haul off and
shoot at Munda. Munda take off running. Then Massa put
Black Nigger on his tail, and Black Nigger like to tore off Munda's leg, and Massa shoot again. This time he kill Munda and
hit Black Nigger in the leg so bad they had to cut it off. And
that's how Massa Higsaw lost his best nigger and a good hunting dog over one wager. And that's how Munda lost his life
for too much hate.

"Unc Steph say to me, 'Boy, don't you never let hate take
you over that way. It ain't no right way to live, and you'll die
in the worship of hate. That Munda was a fool.'"

Luke looked at Daylily. "I's just a little boy when it happened. I heard all the yelling and hollering and shooting, but
I couldn't see nothin. Gustavus say after that, Black Nigger
act like he ain't really living, just a ghost dog, and he lookin
for his leg. Say he be digging up places all over the farm, lookin

for his leg, and don't nobody know where he might be at any time. That Black Nigger dog sure hated niggers, I tell you what."

"What happened to Arkansas?" Daylily asked, turning over to go to sleep under her coat.

"Oh, he never was no good no more. He got whupped for trying to run. And he just sit and stare like a dead man most times. He have a little garden and he just sit. He dead now, bout a year ago at Christmastime. Aunt Eugenia put up a marker for him in the quarters."

CHAPTER 10

GRAN SUSIE'S MICHAEL

The next day Caswell woke up before the others. He was scared to run off now. He was scared all the time. When he was talking to Luke and Daylily, he was scared. When he was staring into the fire, he was scared. Scared of Luke, and scared he'd never see anybody he belonged to again, and scared this girl called Daylily wasn't really nice like she seemed to be. But sometimes, he liked Luke too, except when Luke shouted at him, and then he was scared all over again.

His Mamadear was somewhere else. She wasn't in the fire like that girl said. He didn't believe it. Every day, he felt sick to his stomach. Every night, he cried when nobody was looking, when they thought he was asleep. Sometimes he didn't go to sleep at all. Sometimes he was remembering things, good things that made him get sad and cry. Or bad things that scared him when he thought about it too much, like Michael. Sometimes they told stories, but he couldn't tell this story to Luke and Daylily. He was scared to. They might get mad.

Michael was a slave. Somebody White who was a slave. Mamadear said he was Papa's flesh and blood. He heard her say this behind the library door one day, but he wasn't sure what that meant.

There were things White people could do and things Negras were supposed to do. And there were things Negras were not supposed to do, and things White people were not supposed to do, and sometimes he got them mixed up. His papa told him these were the rules. But Luke acted like he didn't know any of the rules. Luke would have been in trouble back home, and Caswell would have been punished for liking Luke and Daylily the way he did.

He felt bad about going against Papa, so he tried not to like them so much, but he couldn't help it. He was afraid, and they were the only friends he had.

Maybe sometime, he'd ask Luke about Michael. Michael looked like a White boy. Michael couldn't be White though, cause Papa sold him, even though he looked White. He was Gran Susie's boy, he knew that. And Gran Susie was Black. She was a slave. He knew Michael didn't have a daddy.

He remembered standing in the hallway. The hallway had just been waxed by one of the girls. The floors were brown and shiny, and it smelled like wax. If he closed his eyes, he could still smell it. There was a tin bucket sitting there with some wax still in it.

He remembered hearing Papa talking to Gran Susie. Words like *investment* he didn't understand, and Gran Susie said, "Yessuh, yessuh, but he my only chile." And Papa said, "investment" and "business" again, and then Gran Susie came out crying fit to bust and ran to the kitchen.

Before he could move, Mamadear came down the steps and into the library and shut the door, and then it was quiet.

Then he heard Papa say, "Loddy, this is how business works."

And Mamadear said, "Your own flesh and blood! Everybody knows Gran Susie tried to kill herself once. Do you want that to happen?" and something about "going to hell."

Papa said, "those dresses and carpets you love" and "business."

Mamadear said, "Gran Susie's son, Gran Susie's son," louder and louder.

Papa said "hysterical" and "Niggers don't love, they . . ." and then he said a word Caswell didn't understand.

"How dare you speak to me like that!" Mamadear said. "Your wife! Is that how you talk to your Negra women? How many slave wenches do you have? How many?" she shouted.

Then there was a big crash in the room like something broke. And Mamadear was crying and she said, "How many others and which ones?" And then something else broke, and she ran out of the room and back upstairs. And that's when he fell and cut his ear on the tin bucket.

He was scared and he wanted to run up to his Mamadear, but he knew he wasn't supposed to be listening under the stairs. So he ran into the kitchen. He was crying and holding his ear, cause it was bleeding and it hurt bad. Gran Susie was in the kitchen. He didn't want Gran Susie to die. He loved Gran Susie.

Later that night, his Mamadear let him sleep on a pallet in her room, because he had hurt himself, and she asked Gran Susie to sit up with her till she went to sleep because she was upset and didn't want to sleep in the dark alone.

Papa was downstairs smoking cigars. Caswell smelled the cigar smell. Papa never came upstairs till late. Sometimes Caswell would wake up in the night and hear him walking down the long hall.

There was no story or anything that night. And then Mamadear started crying, and she asked Gran Susie to stay with her and not go down to the kitchen where her pallet was. Gran Susie sat in the rocker.

Mamadear said, "You know I know who Michael is." And she said, "How many other girls are there, and who are they?" Mamadear said again louder, "Who are they?" Caswell couldn't see because he was supposed to be asleep, but he heard Gran Susie's rocker squeak three times, and Mamadear said, "Don't make me make you tell."

Gran Susie was whispering then, and she said, "Three that ah knows of, ma'am."

And then Mamadear was quiet, and she cried some more, and then she said, "And who are they and what are their names?"

And Gran Susie rocked some more and she said, "Please, Miz Loddy."

Mamadear said, "I can make you tell me, you know. I can get Overseer Aycock to make you."

And Gran Susie said real low, "Annie, Amelia Ray, and Cestina."

And then Gran Susie's chair was still and Mamadear was crying, and she turned over and cried and cried, and that's all he remembered except he never saw those Negra girls again.

Maybe he'd tell Luke and Daylily about it someday, and ask

what it meant, "flesh and blood." His Mamadear said Michael was Papa's "flesh and blood." Did it mean somebody you loved? And if it did, did Papa love Michael? And why did Michael have to go away from Gran Susie because he was her only child? Maybe Papa was right and Negras didn't love.

CHAPTER 11

LIFE IS BIG

Luke kept at them if they complained of being tired. All he knew was that they had to keep heading north or they'd starve soon. But after a long morning walking, all they wanted to do was sit, Luke included. It was the middle of the day. The sun was high in the sky. Luke stopped and plopped down, and the others followed.

Nobody said anything. Caswell was about to go to sleep, and Luke was thinking. It was a warm day, and the sky was entirely blue. They were resting under the biggest oak tree they had ever seen. It was too hot to sit in the sun. Daylily coughed roughly.

Luke looked at her out of the corner of his eye. This was the third time he had heard her cough, he thought. He thought he had noticed it yesterday.

Luke looked up to the leaves high above them where the sunlight was blinding. It seemed to slide off the leaves of the poplar trees next to Luke and then onto the ground. Luke saw two or three red berries in the brown layers of leaves close to his hand. He checked to see if it was something they could eat, but he didn't recognize the berries. Could be poison, he thought.

Though they had been in the woods for only six days, it felt like forever to him. What worried him most was that he could see little edges of brown just beginning to creep onto a few of the leaves. The hot weather was only Indian summer, Aunt Eugenia used to say.

He knew it could be getting cold now without warning. Unc Steph had taught him to read the weather signs. Fat cat-erpillars, and fat squirrels looking to save nuts meant fall was here. The smell of rotting leaves that had already fallen off the trees was everywhere. It still seemed like summer if you didn't know, but he knew.

All around them were pine, mulberry, poplar and sycamore trees. There were a few large oaks like this one they were sitting under. Except for the meadow in the hot sun up ahead, there were trees as far as they could see. He'd give up his two arms for a cabin with some colored folks in it, a fire, a blanket, and a hot biscuit with some molasses on it.

He'd forgotten what it felt like to be full. They hadn't seen a rabbit since yesterday. He had missed one of the two squir-rels he saw, and they hadn't even seen a house or a barn where there might be some food since they'd left the burnt-out Bur-well place.

He just hoped they were going the right way. On one or two nights he had seen the drinking gourd, but when he got turned around, he couldn't find anything in the sky he could name. He rubbed his sore belly and his thoughts went from one hurting thing to another. He didn't want to think about home. In a minute he was afraid he'd be crying. "Somebody say something," he said.

Daylily made an effort. "Y'all know, back at home, I had lotsa dreams when I got poorly."

"You poorly now," Luke answered, "coughin and wheezin all the time."

She coughed and spit out what came up, and then she leaned against the tree again. "I'm wore out, Luke," she said. "Just plum wore out. That's what Granny would say." She paused and then started again. "I could tell you stories about home," she said. "Bout my folks who took care-a me, to pass the time."

Luke was quiet. Let her talk, he thought. Maybe he wouldn't think so much about biscuits and molasses. He moved around, trying to get comfortable on the ground.

As a soft wind blew, she closed her eyes. Luke knew she was closing her eyes so she could think herself back at the quarters with her granny. He did that too.

In a few seconds, she opened her eyes. "Granny told me lotsa stories. Bout when she was young and pretty. Said she had five husbands. They all dead and left her. One die cause he run away from the massa and she didn't know where he got to, so he gone. She used to pray for him cause she said, 'Every good-bye ain't gone,' but then he never come back, and when she dream he was floating in a river, she know he dead.

"One die from consumption and fever, and one die cause his heart give out from lifting and hauling, one got sold off and one die cause he was in the uprising and he be hanged. Finally, when she left with no husbands the last time, she just say, 'No thank you, Massa, no more. I done had enough of mens dying on me.' And then Granny laugh.

"Granny teach me things too." Daylily stopped, remembering something, and then she said, "Good things."

She had a secret Granny told her never to tell. She sat think-ing about the times she and Granny would be up in the night-time, and Granny would scratch her letters in the dirt floor with a stick. Granny had a little book too, a book she took from Massa's house. She remembered Granny saying, "This here's the Testament. It talk about Master Jesus and how He gon save us Black people from slavery."

But Daylily couldn't tell Luke and Caswell about this. It was a secret.

Granny said they beat her real bad for learning how to read. "See these here scars," she said, and she lifted up her shift. In the firelight, Daylily could see big welts on Granny's old back. "Got these cause Miz Jane teach me to read, and then I got caught learning other folks too."

They would be up most of the night. Granny said she could trust Daylily, and said another beating would kill her for sure. So Daylily never told.

One night Granny whispered to her, "Daylily, reading is like Heaven. Reading will save us Black people one day, you'll see. Words be God's voice. You got to carry on the learning when I'm dead and gone. You keep it going when I'm gone, you hear?"

Daylily's eyes filled up, remembering Granny's voice. "Tell folks life is big. It bigger than this here place. White folks try to keep it secret. That's why they don want us to read. Words make you strong. Words be God's voice. You'll see."

CHAPTER 12

LION

The darkness was coming down so fast it caught them by the nape of the neck. They hadn't collected their wood for the night, they hadn't looked for a safe spot from the rain that might come back in the dark. The last time they had filled their canteens was the night before. There was a little bit of rabbit left from yesterday, and a few pieces of biscuit they had stolen from a farmhouse today.

The biscuits had been sitting in a pan in the window, and they were there for the taking. Luke had inched up to the window, not knowing whether or not someone was in the house. It was a sure thing soldiers had not been there lately, because they would have taken any food left around.

"Look, y'all," said Caswell, "apples." They were all hungry and almost anything looked good. A solitary apple tree near the house had been stripped of all its ripe apples. Just one or two remained, some rotted on the ground, some with worms. Caswell inspected the apples on the ground and bit into one. It was almost too sour to eat.

Daylily was squeamish about eating food that didn't belong to her. Luke whispered that if she was too scared to eat stolen biscuits, she could starve, so she finally took one, and then she stared at it some more as if she couldn't make up her mind.

"Think about it," he said. "Those folks got they kitchens. They can make some more bread. We can't. Tomorrow it be seven days since we been out here. I don't know about you, but I'm hungrier than I ever been."

After that, she gobbled up her share. The dry, crusty bread reminded them all of home.

There was a chopping block near the left side of the house with an ax still stuck in it. "If they ain't here," said Luke, stuffing his mouth, "they be back soon. Nobody would leave a good ax like that out in the weather to rust." They ate in silence and in a hurry, finishing off with sour apples from the tree in the yard.

"Y'all, save some for later," Daylily said. She put two biscuits in her coat pocket, and one in Luke's pocket. Luke was thinking he'd use their well to get water when he looked in the window.

At first he didn't see anyone. "Us better not stay here," he said. "Those folks coming back. Everything in there is as neat as a pin. They close round here somewhere." He looked in the window again. This time he saw a White man asleep on a chair in the shadows.

Just as he said that, the man stirred and stood up. He moved and looked toward the window. Just in time, Luke ducked his head below the windowsill and opened his mouth as if to say, "Run y'all!" But then the man sat down again.

Luke grimaced and waved them away from the window silently. "Whew, that was close," he whispered. "Be real quiet, y'all. Somebody *is* home. And he's a White man. No telling if he's a reb or Union."

They tiptoed away as carefully as they could and then broke into a run. When they thought it was safe again, they slowed to a walk.

"See, I don tole you," Daylily exclaimed. "We shouldn't have stole that man's biscuits!"

"Never mind, you ate em," Luke exclaimed.

"Well . . . yeah" was all Daylily said.

"Got to find us a dry spot," Luke said, breaking into the quiet. There seemed to be mile after mile of trees and flat ground here. No rocks, no caves, nothing to keep out the rain, except the trees. They were in the last few miles before the hills began. He had seen them up ahead this afternoon and knew the hills would lead to the mountains. He had heard the men at home talking about running away, and he knew it was always hills first and then mountains. But here it was all flat, and there was nowhere to hide.

He sat down, worn out, discouraged and hungry, always hungry. He was tired of running, tired of thinking, tired of catching food and stealing food. He wanted Aunt Eugenia, and her warm kitchen, and even her fussing at him. Maybe he should never have left the place after all. Maybe he'd never catch up with anybody he could fight with.

Maybe if he was just by himself, he'd be better off. He could leave, be on his own. He'd have a better chance of finding some Union soldiers if he was without this boy and girl to look after. But then he thought, What would they do without him? Get lost, that's what, and probably die out here.

Daylily could see something was wrong. "Come on, Luke,"

she said brightly. "Us got to plan for the night. It coming on night fast."

"You plan," he said. "I's tired and I's gonna sleep right here." And he spread out his old jacket on the leaves.

She didn't want to upset him. She didn't want to make him mad at her. She couldn't stand to think about being alone.

Caswell sat nearby, looking sleepy and about to fall over under a tree. She went and took him by the hand. "You need to do something?" she said.

He shook his head.

"Don't be wetting your trousers," she told him. "You been good so far. And you ain't got no more. If you wet your pants, you be cold over in the night."

He shook his head again as if to say, no, I won't.

She led him over to Luke, put both their coats down and said, "Lie down. Sleep time." Caswell obeyed. She put herself down next to him and pulled her coat over both of them.

Around midnight, Luke stirred. He sat up, realizing that he had not made a fire. They were in the deepest darkness he could imagine. He shivered and wrapped his coat more tightly around his legs.

They just had to run into some Union soldiers soon. He was so homesick for Aunt Eugenia that he had dreamed about her. And, he had been dreaming about his mama. He could feel her face bending over him, smell her as if she was really there, but he didn't see her face in his dreams ever.

He remembered the creek she told him about when he was little. The creek where she went to bathe and where she felt like a lady. That was before his mam went bad in the head.

Aunt Eugenia had told him something about a plan some folks had to run away, and then Massa killed his mam cause somebody told him she was gonna take her boy and run. Aunt Eugenia said it was not right for friends to tell on each other. They were supposed to look out for each other. He tried to remember the story. It would help him to stay awake. He was terribly sleepy, and his head bobbed every few minutes.

Then he'd be awake and look around, afraid of wild things, afraid of soldiers too, or stragglers. He heard a rustle in the leaves. Some mouse or possum on the prowl, he thought.

He should get some wood to make a fire. But that would mean leaving Daylily and Caswell alone. He was scared to move, and scared not to move. He tried to think himself into a warm piece of fatback and greens from the pot. And then that hurt his stomach and he couldn't think of food anymore. Mam was better. He'd try to remember her face.

All he could usually remember was how it felt to stand with her skirt wrapped around his face and her mama smell. And how she said, "Take care of your friends, Luke baby. A friend is a blessing from the Lord in this evil world." He could almost hear her saying it. He tried to remember her laughing. She had a high thin laugh.

She used to think he was a funny boy. Told him he was smart *and* funny, and to be careful cause White folks didn't like that in a Black person. He closed his eyes real tight so he could remember his mam before her sickness in the head came on. He could feel her hands scrubbing his face clean, washing his arms. It made him sad that he couldn't remember her face.

Somewhere in this remembering he realized that something was moving near them. At first he heard it only in that part of him that said it wasn't so. And then he knew it was so. There was no fire and no wood near him. Something coming closer. Luke picked up his rifle. Thank you, Jesus, he thought, it was loaded and ready.

Leaves cracked and rustled, and the moist smell under them reached up to Luke's nostrils. He could smell everything— their sour clothes, mold and decaying trees—and he could even see outlines of rocks and bushes in the dark. His sweat smelled like salt. Unc Steph had said animals could smell fear on you. He could taste his own saliva.

Where was the thing? He didn't dare move. Caswell murmured in his sleep about Mamadear. Luke was too far away to hush him up. God, please God, he prayed. Don't let him start whining and get up.

Then he saw them. Two yellow eyes through the underbrush. He was afraid whatever it was could hear his heart, it was beating so fast. The angels, the god of winds, some good something blew across the moon and uncovered it. And now he could see it was a mountain lion. The light brown fur, the pointed ears, the arched back. They stared at each other.

. Luke knew with a country boy's instinct that the thing would attack if it was afraid. The cat had probably come down out of the mountains to find food. If it was hungry, it would be bold. He waited, praying, "Lord Jesus . . . ," trying to remember what Aunt Eugenia had told him about praying, but he could only remember, "Oh, Lord Jesus, oh, Lord Jesus," so he said that over and over.

The big cat started over toward Caswell, slowly sniffing, not desperate, only mildly interested in human aroma. It gave Luke a chance to lift his rifle and get ready to fire.

Caswell whimpered. If he fired and missed, Caswell would be a dead boy. The cat sniffed again. Something in his body told Luke there was no more time. He knew if Caswell woke up with that cat in his eyes, he would holler and bring death down on all of them. He fired.

The explosion echoed violently, ringing through the dark woods, a hawk shrieked somewhere, leaves trembled and fell, and startled birds went crashing through the foliage. For once, Massa Higsaw had done something good, and he didn't even know it. He had probably saved three children by teaching Luke about guns. The cat screamed in a death dance and fell on top of Caswell. The smell of the cat's blood rushed out into the dark.

Daylily cried out and at the same time, Luke was trying to load the rifle again, packing it with his musket ball, but it wasn't necessary. The cat was dead.

Luke pulled the hysterical Caswell out from under the cat's belly, and while the little boy clung to him and wailed, and Daylily hung on to his neck, Luke realized he was glad Caswell was alive, really glad. He was awfully glad Daylily was alive too.

Glad they were together in the lonesome forest, where, truth be told, nobody knew for sure if they'd ever come home again anywhere, or see anybody they called family. He felt they were all kin now. And right then in the middle of the trees under the moonlight, with the smell of dead mountain lion and pines all mingling together, he was sure he knew what his mama had meant when she said, "Take care of your friends, Luke baby. A friend is a blessing from the Lord in this evil world."

CHAPTER 13

FEVER

On the eighth day, they walked until close to sunset, still following the river on their left. Trees were not as thick as they had been on the right, and there was a farm in the distance, but on the other side of the river were trees thick as ever, and also there was a peculiar-looking hill. From where they stood, Luke saw a small cave or maybe a place that had been dug out in the dirt on the side of the hill, and sticks laid across the dugout, like somebody had made a place to sit out of the rain.

"Can you swim, Daylily?" Luke asked, looking at the river. She shook her head violently.

"Not me."

"I can swim," Luke assured her. "I can save you. You swim, Caswell?" Caswell moved his head up and down slowly.

Dalylily said, "You lying, you can't do no such thing."

"Can too," insisted Caswell, his small chin sticking out as far as it could go. He was determined to prove himself. "You don't know anything about what I can do!"

"Us should cross over," Luke said, pointing to the place in the hill that looked like a perfect campsite. The river was not deep here, and there was a fallen tree that formed a perfect bridge. "This is what us gon do. Us can use that log for a bridge."

Daylily peered sideways at him. She didn't like this, but a place to stretch out and rest sounded wonderful, and she still didn't feel good. She was tired and hungry. They could make a fire there. She nodded her agreement. She was to go first and then Caswell, then Luke so he could watch them both and hang on to Caswell's pants to make sure he didn't fall in. The log was wet and looked slippery, but nobody thought about sitting down and scooting until it was too late. It looked like it'd be easy.

The log seemed wide enough to walk. Daylily stepped out on the log, but she was suddenly as stiff as a tree, and her legs wouldn't work for her. She was scared to move. The cold water running under the dead tree had her hypnotized.

"Hurry up," Luke yelled. "Hurry up!" You makin it harder! Just walk natural like you goin cross a field!"

But she couldn't look down into the bubbling water without getting dizzy. The water looked as deep as the well back at the Riversons' place. If she drowned, would she go to Heaven? Then all at once, rigid with fear, she was over the side into the river.

"Hold on to the log!" Luke screamed. "Hold on to the log, it ain't deep!" The water was shallow, but it was fast moving, and she was fighting for her life with her eyes closed.

Luke jumped the last two feet onto the bank, holding Caswell around the waist, and set him down on the ground. Daylily was already three or four feet downriver, sputtering, arms fighting the water with every gasp for air.

"Stand up!" Luke was screaming. He threw off his coat and jumped in trying to get to her. "It ain't deep! Stand up!"

She finally heard him and found the bottom. Still close to the bank, Daylily saw that land was within reach, started toward it and fell again. The heavy waterlogged coat she was wearing pulled her down. She reached out for an overhanging branch before Luke could get to her and pulled herself up. As soon as they saw she was all right, Luke and Caswell broke out laughing. They were all hysterical with relief.

Daylily's hair dripped into her eyes, and the heavy coat streamed with river water. She lay on the riverbank, coughing and laughing. Crying and sputtering, too exhausted to move. "Ooh, Lordy," she said, "I thought I was a goner for sure!" She suddenly realized how wet she was between coughing and spitting up water. "Got to get out of these wet clothes. It be cold now. Night comin on."

"Silly gal, I told you to stand up! Givin me and Caswell such a turn! Wouldn't that be somethin!" Luke laughed, taking off his wet shoes. "Drownin in two feet of water! You take my coat," he said. "I'll make the fire. Come on, Caswell, us got to hurry!"

Luke walked off barefoot, moving like someone used to walking in the woods with no shoes. The trousers would dry in the breeze before nightfall. Stripped down to her shirtwaist, Daylily wrapped up in Luke's coat.

The cave they thought they had seen was really a small indented place in a hillside. Luke went first to check it. He walked slowly to the dugout. And now he could see there was more than one. Soldiers been here, he thought. They dug these places in the side of the hill, just big enough to lie down in or maybe to load a gun. He could see where wooden boards had been put up to keep the dirt from falling in.

"Don't y'all come any closer," he called to them. "Wait there for me." He walked around a little farther on the other side of the hill. Inside the dugout on the ground was a pile of old rotten cloth. He kicked at it. And then he gasped and covered his mouth with his hands. It was a human skull. Then he could see there was more. A whole soldier's skeleton, someone left dead a long time ago, maybe when the war had started two or three years before. He backed away silently. He could hear Daylily calling him.

"Luke, where you?"

"I'm comin," he yelled shakily. "I'm comin." When he got back to where they were standing, he lied. "Nothin round there. Let me look in here," and he walked into the first dugout they had seen. It was empty and dry. "This is good," he said. "We can stay here tonight."

By the time they had a fire going, night crickets were starting up and the waning moon was showing behind some clouds. They could hear the Shenandoah flowing over the rocks. At least Luke hoped it was the Shenandoah; that's what he'd heard folks called the river that ran through the mountains. If it was the Shenandoah, that would mean they were in Virginia, and that would mean they were closer to the north. It should be Virginia by now, he thought. They had been walking for eight days.

Luke's shoes were propped up on some stones near the fire. Daylily slept heavily in Luke's coat, and he stuck three dead branches into the ground and draped her coat and dress over them, facing the fire. He took a small piece of soggy, leftover fish from his pocket and divided it with the younger boy.

Daylily coughed under his jacket. The sound of her coughing came and went, but it was gentle. An owl hooted, and Luke thought about bears and wondered if there were any in this part of the woods. These woods were pretty thick.

Caswell whispered, "Luke, you know any more stories? Gran Susie used to tell me stories. She used to tell about the mud turtle and about the rabbit." He had stretched out on his coat on his stomach.

"Don't know no mud turtle," Luke muttered.

"I can't sleep," Caswell whined. "Sweetbriar could tell sto-ries too," he said wistfully. His eyes filled with tears, and he wiped his face with the back of his hand and left a streak of dirt on his cheek.

"All right, don't tune up," said Luke. "Guess what? I knew a story about a White slave boy once had pink eyes and white skin. You don't wanna hear it though—you be scared." Luke's long legs stretched out toward the fire, and he scratched an itch on his elbow.

"I won't," Caswell retorted.

"Aw, shoot, Caswell, you be scared if I tell you that out here in the dark."

"I won't be!" Caswell answered. He sat up on his coat. "If he's White, he can't be a slave. I know better. You just try me. Tell it, Luke; I wanna hear it."

"Well," Luke started, "was a boy on the place."

Daylily turned and coughed again in her sleep.

Luke looked quickly in her direction before continuing. "Boy on the place I come from? Us called him Pink Eye. Say his mama was a cat cause-a them eyes." Luke looked at Cas-well's face.

Caswell was paying very close attention.

"Everybody say his mama was a cat, cause he didn't have

no mama that us knew about. Pink Eye lived with Buster and Jim Jim in they cabin long as I know him. And you know what?"

"What?" Caswell said, leaning forward.

"He's white as you and he's a slave," said Luke. "I swear it's the truth. White, white skin, and yaller nappy hair. And far's I know that ole Pink Eye's a slave today."

"I knew somebody like that," Caswell said. "His name is Michael. He *looked* like a White boy, but he was really Black. I know cause my daddy sold him, and you can't sell White people. There aren't any White slaves, are there? You must be joshing me, aren't you, Luke? And nobody has a cat for a mama!"

Daylily coughed a little louder.

Luke looked over at her. "He still a slave," Luke said. "Massa Higsaw sold him down the river to New Orleans. Slave trader say he buying freaks for a freak show. Gon show him as a nigger boy with a white cat for a mama. Ole Pink Eye. Now go on to sleep. That's all my story. Be quiet. Us got to listen for bears."

At the mention of bears, Caswell lay down wide awake. Luke stretched out as near as he could to the fire, with one hand on the rifle. He tried very hard to keep his eyes open, but he kept losing the struggle. After a few minutes they all dozed. All through the night Luke would nod and wake up, and nod and wake up.

Daylily's cough got more and more frequent and more and more rough. Once in the middle of the night she sat up and looked around wildly, and then fell back into sleep. Luke woke up all the way, suddenly startled. Then he realized what had awakened him. It was Daylily's cough. He remembered hear-

ing sick folks in the quarters when they got the croup. That's
the way it sounded. He remembered his mama told him Miss
Barbara's baby had died of the croup. Aunt Eugenia said that
was when Luke was a baby, died in twenty-four hours.

Luke got up and felt Daylily's head like Aunt Eugenia used
to do when he was sick. He knew that if it was hot, that was
bad. Daylily had thrown back his coat and was exposed to the
dew in only her shirtwaist and bloomers. She was crying out
in little yelps and squeaks. "No," she said, and "no" again.

Luke didn't know much about doctoring folks, but he knew
she was really bad off. Her face was as hot as his got from the
fire's heat, only now the fire was just smoldering coals. He
pulled the coat around her again. She should have some tea,
some soup, something to drink.

He had watched Aunt Eugenia tend to folks enough to
know that. She used to grind up some kind of leaves to make
a tea. He set himself the task of finding something that looked
like the herbs he had seen his aunt use. In the firelight he could
just barely see that creecy greens were growing wild a few feet
from them.

Luke looked for his canteen and poured a little water in the
cup. He tore a few of the greens into small pieces and put them
in as well, and put the cup on the hot coals. Then he woke
Caswell up and sent him to gather twigs to build up the fire.
In a few minutes the tea was warm, pieces of the leaves floating in it.

"Come on, gal," he coaxed, "you got to eat somethin." Her
face was damp. She smelled like sickness to him. "Just a little
somethin; come on now."

Daylily's eyes opened slightly; she turned her head away
from Luke's face. "Granny," she mumbled.

"Now come on," he insisted, feeling desperate and forcing her head around to the cup. She knocked the cup onto the ground. Her tangled hair was wet with sweat, and her dark brown eyes were ringed with darker circles.

"Now see what you done," Luke chided. "You more stubborn sick than you is well." He wanted to cry. The fish from yesterday was all gone, she had wasted the drink he had made and he couldn't get anything much into her mouth from his canteen. It kept dribbling down her chest. She had lost her canteen cup when she fell in the water. And her hat too. At least her dress had dried in front of the fire. "We got to get this dress over her head," he said to Caswell. She was still making little noises and flinging her arms around. "Stop looking so scared, Caswell, and come over here and help me."

Caswell was almost frozen with fear. His mouth was open, but nothing was coming out.

"Just set up now," Luke said, trying to calm her. "Got to put on your dress. Us ain't goin to hurt you." Luke raised her up gently. She seemed almost asleep, but she wouldn't be still. He motioned again to Caswell to come nearer, and together they stretched the little cotton frock over her head and pulled it down as far as they could.

Then Luke had an idea. He took the carved figurine, his mam's mojo, that he was wearing, and laid it gently over her head and around her neck. He thought it would be all right with his mam, and maybe it would help Daylily.

Caswell looked at the wooden carving on her neck. "You oughtn't to put that devil's charm on her," he said to Luke. Before he could get any more words out of his mouth, Luke had grabbed his arm and dragged him a few feet away from the sleeping girl.

"You hurting me, Luke," he whimpered. "Let me go!" He tried to pull his arm away from Luke.

"What you callin a devil's charm was my mam's mojo." Luke's voice was low and deadly serious. His words came out like they were squeezed through his teeth. He held on to Caswell's shoulder. "You try to take it off or even touch it, I'll fix you so you can't see or talk, ever. You hear me? All I got to do is pray over that mojo and you be 'fixed.' So you keep your mouth shut about my mam. You hear me? Now I got to try to get some water into that gal." He went to get his canteen and left Caswell standing in silence, afraid to argue or even move from that spot.

At dawn, Luke tried again to get a few drops of water into Daylily's mouth from her canteen. All that hot and muggy day he fed her drops of water and tried to keep the bugs off her. Mosquitoes were the worst, and she was sweating from her fever. She would lick the water from around her mouth and cry out for Granny.

Just when he couldn't stand it any more, he remembered sassafras. That's what he needed. Something that would cure the shaking and burning up of fever. If only he could remember what it looked like.

He called Caswell to watch her and went looking for the herbs again. He had to find them before night came. "Call out for me if she tries anything," he ordered. "And don't you move a muscle from her. Try to keep her cool, and fan her with your hand, like this." He showed Caswell what to do and headed into the wooded area.

Luke thought he might know it if he saw it, but he couldn't get too far from the others. He made a wide circle around them, never out of earshot. "Poison oak in these woods," he mumbled to himself. "That's all I been seeing, more and more poison oak, and wild strawberries." He picked some of them, thinking that they might be good for her too.

First all he could find was dandelion, and he knew they could eat those leaves. But one of them healing plants, he thought, had purple flowers with yellow in the center. Purple cornflower, Aunt Eugenia called it. But sassafras was the one she liked better. What did it look like? Then he remembered. The mitten, the mitten leaves. That's what she said was good for sickness. If he could just find some!

When he heard Daylily cough, he was about to give up and go back when he looked straight ahead. He was standing right in front of it. Green mitten leaves! He grabbed some leaves and peeled a small piece of bark. Now he could get her well, he thought. Now she'd be all right. He made some sassafras tea, warming the leaves in his cup, and gave her a sip.

Luke could feel himself getting very hungry. They had to have more fish because they had to eat. Even if she died, he reckoned they had to eat even though he didn't want to say it even to himself. "Caswell," he said, "you got to dig for some bait. You know what that is?"

Caswell seemed to be glad to help. "I used to go fishing with Daniel," he said. "I can dig for worms."

Luke needed the line and hook they had made. Oh, God, let it be in her pocket, he thought, and not at the bottom of the river. He stopped feeding Daylily tea long enough to look inside her coat pocket. The inside of the pocket was still damp, but he felt something sharp. The pin she had bent stuck him. He had never been so glad to prick his finger on anything.

Caswell took the bayonet and dug in the soft dirt near the

water. Normally digging for worms might have been fun, but now it was just something he had to do.

"Got one," he said in a minute or two, holding up a wiggling worm.

"Good, give it here," Luke said, intent on catching fish.

Luke caught two small fish and cooked them. They ate, and then he made some more sassafras tea and gave Daylily sip after sip. But she seemed to get worse, talking out loud about things they didn't understand, and she tried to sing something about "angels Black like me."

Once, she tried to take off her coat, and once, she vomited up her tea. Then she tried to get up, and they had to hold her down. Luke was close to tears and Caswell was already crying. She was sweating and her eyes were big and bright, too bright, Luke thought.

"Naw, gal, naw," Luke pleaded desperately. "Look, I'll sing to you, how bout that? I'll sing you a song about Heaven, about tryin to make Heaven my home." Through his tears, Caswell said, "I know that one! Gran Susie sings that to me!"

"See, see? Even Caswell know that one, don't you, Caswell?"

Caswell nodded. And so they sang a few words, and hummed to her because they forgot all the words they were taught, except for "I am a poor pilgrim of sorrow; I'm tossed on this wide world alone; I've heard of a city called Heaven; I've started to make it my home." And they sang that over and over, until she got quiet.

They held her in their arms, one of them on each side of her. Finally, Daylily quieted down and closed her eyes, and it seemed they had sung her back to sleep.

"Oh, Lordy," Luke sighed when they could finally rest. He stretched out on his stomach by the fire and put his head down in his arms. Caswell sat down next to him.

"Luke," Caswell said, looking into the fire, "is she gonna die?"

He didn't answer for several seconds. Caswell had to repeat the question, his eyes bewildered and terrified. "Is she gonna die, Luke? Luke?"

"Maybe," the older boy whispered, almost to himself. He didn't raise his head.

Caswell whimpered.

"Shut up!" Luke hissed, finally looking at Caswell. "Can't nobody deal with you cryin at a time like this. Maybe so, maybe not! Just shut up!"

Look like that mojo should be working better than this, Luke thought. For a while there was silence except for animal sounds and the crackling of the fire. He guessed he could pray some. He thought about Preacher Brown in the quarters back home. He would know how to pray for Daylily. Luke bowed his head and prayed the best way he could. Mostly he whispered, "Oh, Lord, please make Daylily well" over and over.

That night wore on forever. Luke was so scared and so tired that he finally asked Caswell if he wanted to hear another story, just to pass the time, so that for a few minutes, he wouldn't have to think about Daylily over there coughing, maybe dying, but Caswell had dropped off to sleep. Luke gave her some more tea, then pulled the almost-dried-out and smelly soldier's coat around himself and dropped down close enough to her to grab her if she tried to get up during the night. Finally, his exhaustion took over, and as hard as he tried to stay awake, he couldn't, and he slept.

Luke heard a voice say, "You seven. Seven years good luck, Luke. You the one chile I got to keep." There was a hole in the door where he liked to look through and sometimes stick his finger. This time an ant crawled up the door. It was night and there was a moon out now. He saw a woman in the cornfield callin, "Jesus, Jesus." He heard a voice that said, "Come on in, come on in now." Then he saw somebody's red back and he heard his mama say, "Please, Massa, please, Massa," and then he saw her legs in the dust. He ran and ran, trying to find Aunt Eugenia, and then it was dark, black dark, and he heard a gunshot . . .

He woke up sweating in his coat and felt for his mojo, but it was gone. For a minute he didn't know where it was, and his heartbeats fluttered like leaves in a storm. Then he remembered he had put it on Daylily. He sat up fully awake, scared that maybe she was dead, and maybe that was why he had had that dream again.

Daylily looked at him and said, in a weak little voice, "Hey, Luke, what's this here thing roun my neck?"

Little pieces of her hair were stuck up all over her head, and her cotton dress was a mess, but she looked wonderful to Luke; he knew she was going to be all right, and maybe it was the mojo, and maybe it was the praying, but it didn't matter to him.

The next day they stayed put. She was feeling better and she thought they should move on, but Luke said no. It was hard for Daylily to be still without anything to do. Caswell tried working on his aim by knocking down his tin cup with stones, and Luke was down at the water's edge filling their canteens.

"Lord knows I am ready to leave here," she sighed. She was lying on her coat in the sun.

"You ain't well yet," Luke called to her over her shoulder.

Daylily was looking around for her canteen to get a drink when she saw Luke had taken it to the river's edge. She got to her feet and slowly made her way to the riverbank. She was almost there when everything swirled in front of her eyes and her knees buckled under her.

Luke heard her hit the ground. "Tarnation!" Luke yelled. "Girl, what you trying to do, kill yourself?"

She opened her eyes slowly. "What happened?" she whispered.

Caswell ran over to them from where he had been throwing stones. "You fainted," he cried, "just like my Mamadear used to."

"That does it," said Luke, helping her stand up. "We ain't going nowhere till tomorrow. Come on, you going back and lie down."

The next day they fed her little bits of rabbit and fish, whatever Luke could catch. He knew for sure Daylily was getting well when she wanted her fishing hook and line again and started telling him he didn't know how to fish. He was so glad that all he did was grin.

CHAPTER 14

A CURVE IN
THE ROAD

Once Daylily was better, they could move ahead. They were still in the woods, but they were a little closer to the troop lines. Luke could tell because they were beginning to hear guns, not loud but in the distance. Luke said aloud, "It's them guns again, no doubt about it."

They began to see signs of people too—a Union cap that somebody had dropped in the mud, a muddy pair of gloves. Caswell lagged behind them. He had seen something he was curious about under the bushy growth. He stuck his hand under the bush and grabbed it. It was a single boot, cut open with dried blood caked all inside. He threw it down because it had spooked him.

Luke turned around just in time to see Caswell stick something in his pocket, but he forgot about it, because just then Daylily found a tin of chewing tobacco.

The weather was holding good, and they caught some fish in the river. After they ate, they felt a little better, at least Luke and Caswell did.

Daylily didn't seem to be getting any better than she had been a couple of days before when they'd started walking again. Her sickness was slowing them down. Sometimes Luke carried Caswell on his back, because his being so little slowed them down even more.

Both Luke and Daylily were beginning to get sore places where the too-big shoes rubbed on their feet, but it was better than wearing no shoes at all. They had been wearing these shoes for more than a week. Luke counted on his fingers. Eleven days now since he'd left the home place. It seemed like forever, and he was getting really tired.

They sat on the banks of the river that was widening, and Daylily watched the water bubbling over the rocks. There were lots and lots of rocks. "I sure would love to bathe in there," she said, "specially my feet. They killing me. That water would feel specially good. I don't wanna get in it, you understand. Just my feet. Look, Luke, it ain't deep at all."

"It's too deep," Luke said, "and it's rough. It's river water. Can't depend on river water. Might get mean on you before you know it. You drown or somethin, and you still coughin anyway."

She pouted. But Luke had a terrible fear that she would die and leave him to deal with Caswell and getting out of the woods, and he couldn't stand the thought of that. She kept that coughing up every day, and she looked peaked.

"Maybe tomorrow," he said. "You still look poorly. Eat the rest of your fish," he said like a mother. Her eyes still looked too big to Luke, and her arms as little as twigs. They had to reach the Union lines soon before something awful happened. He began to gather wood for the night.

Daylily took one bite. "I ain't hungry," she said. "Here, Caswell, you eat it." Daylily wandered a few feet away. "Look here," she said, looking at some old ashes and burnt wood.

Caswell was busy eating her fish so he didn't pay any attention. "Somebody done made a fire. Wonder if they be comin
back"

"Naw, this a old campground," Luke said. "Trees a little
thinner here. Close to the water. Could-a been from soldiers,
or just folks wanderin through. Look at them ashes. They been
rained on more than once." He threw some wood down and
went to get more. Come to think of it, Luke thought, Caswell
didn't look too good either, scrawny little arms, blond hair all
matted and dirty. I'm getting worse than Aunt Eugenia, he
said to himself. Worryin bout young'uns all the time. Finally
he had enough wood for the night.

In a few minutes, Daylily was fast asleep. She slept a lot
and talked less and less now. Caswell got up to chase fireflies
winking on and off. The last of the season. Suddenly he stood
still. "Luke," he asked, looking at the last of the sunset, "you
reckon my Mamadear can see me from way up there in them
clouds?"

Luke nursed their little fire along. He looked at the small
child. He knew what Caswell was feeling. His mama gone, he
thought. Luke thought of Lucymae, his own Mamadear in
Heaven. He knew for certain she had to be there. Otherwise
he'd just lie down right here by this ole river and die. Cause
somebody had to see you, somebody sure did, or you wasn't
really alive.

He looked at Caswell like he was really seeing him for the
first time. He couldn't stand no more death, no more pain.
Caswell looked at Luke, really trusting him to tell the truth.

"You listen to me, Caswell," said Luke, pointing his finger
at the little boy. "All we got right now is us—you, me and
Daylily. We's all the family we got. So we's all got to stay

alive. You hear me? And yes, your Mamadear is up there. She know you here with us and want you to grow up and be a good man. You hear me? She up there lookin down at you and don't you never forget it."

Caswell nodded and looked out into the sunset. He was tryin to see his Mamadear in the clouds. "She's up there," he kept saying. "She's up there." And then he lay down on his coat. The sun went out of sight, Daylily coughed, and Luke sighed and put some more wood on the fire. In a few minutes, Caswell was asleep. Time went by very slowly. Luke stretched out on the ground. He was exhausted and wondered how all this would end. He was hungry all the time and cold every night, and just now he felt like giving up.

In the dark, Luke could hear the gurgling water and eve-ning insects. And then somehow he knew there was somebody or something there. He didn't really hear or see anything, he just knew it. Luke sat up very slowly, completely alert. He had left his bayonet and rifle on the other side of the fire. Luke swore under his breath like a man.

Then he heard a twig break and saw something come out of the trees. It had been right in front of them. The light from the fire and shadows made strange patterns everywhere. At first Luke didn't know if it was a man or a woman. He was terrified. His heart was pounding in his ears. He was afraid to move. Then the firelight shown on her face, and Luke saw a woman with two long braids, in a long dirty dress and an army cap. She stood still and looked at him and didn't say anything.

He saw the beads around her neck in the firelight, but he was too scared to say anything. She carried a rifle. Daylily coughed again.

The woman pointed to Daylily and said, "Sick."

He nodded. He thought of haints and spirits in the woods. Mostly he thought of his bayonet on the other side of the fire. He could barely swallow, but he could hear Daylily's rough breathing and thought it was his own.

The woman walked over to Daylily and touched her face. Luke stood up and went after the woman, but before he could hit her, she had hold of his arms. The beads swayed down across the woman's heavy breasts. "You wait, wait," she said fiercely, holding him as he struggled. She was very strong. "She got the smell of death on her. You need good medicine fast!"

Luke heard the word *death* and stood stock-still. The mysterious woman looked him in the eye. "You lost?"

He breathed in and out in ragged spurts. Something felt like it was coming apart inside of him piece by piece. "We goin north" was all that he could think to answer her. She had touched Daylily without harming her, and she looked like somebody's grandmother. He could see that now, familiar lines in her face, the gray hair. He calmed down a little, but his nut-brown face was wet with tears.

Just as he thought the word, *grandmother*, the woman swooped down on Daylily and scooped her up. "Come," she said to Luke. "We go to my place. I have good medicine. Food. Bring the little one." But she could see he did not want to leave their precious coats and rifle and canteens. "Stay here," she said. "I comin back."

He couldn't let her take Daylily away, and he couldn't leave Caswell. All he could do was sit down, helpless and confused. He wiped his face with his sleeve.

Losing their coats and rifle would be the end of them. What

if she was a spirit, and he never saw Daylily again? But she had said "medicine" and "food," the things they needed so much.

It was very quiet now. Their fire was burning down. All he could hear was the running stream, Caswell's breathing and crickets. This old woman had Daylily, and she had disappeared into the trees without a sound. He peered into the darkness, but it was as deep as a cave. Should he wake Caswell, get their things and try to find Daylily? Just as he had finally decided he'd have to do that, she appeared without Daylily, picked up the little boy and said, "Bring your things, this way."

He scrambled to get their coats. The woman walked fast, and they were in thick woods. He could barely hear her quiet steps in the dark, and before he knew it they came to a cabin. They had been only a few feet away from her when they'd stopped for the night. If they had gone a little farther, they would have seen the house. She stepped through the small door and put Caswell on something narrow and low. There was a warm fire in the cabin.

"Sit. I fix the fire," she said, pointing outside, and she disappeared again, going in the direction of their campfire.

Luke looked around nervously. Her little house was mostly one room, a big fireplace, and lots and lots of stuff everywhere. In the shadows, he couldn't make out what was stacked up in the corners. It took him a few minutes to see two dogs sleeping in one corner of the cramped space. They didn't look very mean, but you never could tell about dogs. On the floor, under a blanket hanging on the wall, were three folded quilts. There was a big loom on the opposite wall.

The door to the cabin opened silently, and the woman walked over to the fire and stirred something in a pot that he could smell. He hadn't eaten good food in so long that it made his stomach feel strange, and he was slow knowing just how good it smelled. He felt light in the head all of a sudden.

She put a bowl and a wooden spoon under his nose. Luke stood up and let go of all their things. He grabbed the bowl from her and began to stuff himself before he thought about what he was doing.

"Sit down," she said, "sit," and motioned to the floor in front of the fire.

Luke ate the whole bowl standing up; he almost choked on a piece of meat. She looked at him, tilting her head.

"Betty Strong Foot will give you more," she said in a low voice. "There is more meat. Too much too fast will make you sick."

Luke finally sat down after he finished licking the bowl like a puppy. He was sleepy but afraid to go to sleep. This woman might be dangerous. He couldn't tell if she was colored or not. She looked different to him. He could see she wasn't very light, and her hair was really long. For all he knew she had put poison in that bowl.

Daylily turned over and murmured something in her sleep. Maybe if he was polite, she would be nice to them. He finally spoke. "Thank you, ma'am. My name Luke."

"In the morning *they* eat," the woman said. She was mixing up something in a round bowl with a big stick. "Medicine for the girl. What's her name?"

He was so sleepy. It took him a long time to answer. He felt like a ghost to himself. Finally, he said, "Her name Daylily." And then he fell over slowly on the floor into the deepest sleep he could ever remember.

CHAPTER 15

PROMISE AND
APPLE PIE

Betty Strong Foot wasn't there when the dawn came. Luke woke up startled, thinking at first he had had a dream about a strange woman, but after his eyes were all the way opened, he remembered. It was true, it had really happened! He shook Daylily and Caswell. "Hey, y'all! Hey!" He was whispering just in case she was lurking around there behind those boxes. "Wake up!"

Daylily stared at Luke and then at Caswell. "Luke," she whispered, "where we at?" Caswell just looked at the older ones, waiting for an answer to this latest catastrophe.

"We need to get gone," Luke said, looking over his shoulder. "This here woman lives in this house. She gave me somethin that made me real sleepy. Maybe she a hoodoo woman. She fixin to. . . ." Suddenly he sensed she had come up behind him silent as snow. Daylily and Caswell each grabbed one of his arms.

"Daylily sick," said Betty Strong Foot. "To go is not good. Sit still. Your food is coming." Caswell was so scared his eyes were as big as plates, and Daylily looked at Luke for help.

"This here's Betty Strong Fingers," he said to Daylily.

"Foot," the woman corrected him.

"Sorry, ma'am, . . . and she took us out the woods." He could see now that she was as brown as he was. So, she wasn't White, he wasn't dead and she didn't poison him. She had thick, long braids that were not straight but not kinky either. He still thought they should plan their escape, but he didn't want Betty to know that. "And she give me some meat and . . ."

Betty was holding a clay bowl. "You drink this medicine," she said to the girl. "It'll make you well."

It was full of some greenish water. Daylily looked at Luke for permission.

He thought about the meat. "OK," he whispered, "it's OK." Daylily made a terrible face, gagged and swallowed it.

"Now we gonna eat," said Betty. She motioned for them all to sit on the dirt floor. Caswell and Daylily crowded together, almost on top of each other trying to get next to Luke. They were all silent. Betty handed out bowls with some kind of meat and corn cakes. They all held their bowls, but nobody started to eat.

Now that they were inside and it was day, Luke realized how poorly the other two looked, and he wondered if he looked as sick as they did. They really needed this food. He fingered his mojo and prayed silently that they wouldn't all die from her breakfast. She ate out of the same big pot, so he figured it was safe. As Luke reached for his meat, Caswell began to eat. Daylily just looked at her food.

Betty Strong Foot said, "Must eat to get well." Luke nudged Daylily with his elbow, and motioned for her to eat. She took one bite of the meat, and one bite of the corn cake and chewed it very slowly.

• • •

For three days, Betty made them wash their sore and blistered feet in the nearby river, smeared their feet with some kind of oil, and wrapped them in rags. She cooked soup and bread and told stories. She told them the name of this river was the Shenandoah and that it meant "sisters of the stars." And if you kept going, the river got much bigger. She said her daddy was Black like Daylily and Luke, and her mama was a Seminole Indian. "White folks call me half-breed. But I ain't half anything," she said.

And she listened to their stories one at a time. Luke talked about how he had run away to fight with the Union, and Caswell talked about his Mamadear. Betty rocked Caswell to sleep in her rocking chair, and after that, Caswell followed her around like she was his Gran Susie.

Only Daylily wouldn't tell much, and she didn't want to stay there, even though she did feel better. Her chest had almost stopped hurting, and she didn't have the misery in her head. By the third day, she stopped sleeping all the time, and she was eating almost all her food. But she didn't trust this Indian woman who called her "Mouth-Stuck-Together," and she was afraid of her.

At night she would whisper to Luke about how she was scared of Betty's house and that she thought it was full of haints. All those baskets and balls of old cloth, wooden boxes in the shadows, and clothes piled up could be hiding something. Daylily thought they should get out of there.

Only Luke was not sure he wanted to go yet. He was glad to be warm and full, and he kept thinking about what it was like back in the woods.

On the fourth afternoon, when Daylily was a lot stronger,

Betty fixed her eyes on Daylily and said, "Come with me. We gotta get plants for your medicine. Good medicine for bad sickness in the woods."

Luke looked at Daylily. She was staring at her feet. "I'll go with you, Miz Betty," said Luke. "She don't feel too good."

Betty shook her head. "Only girls can do this. Watch the little one." She took an old basket off the back door and hooked it on her arm. "You come," she said to Daylily, and started out the door.

"Go!" Luke whispered fiercely. "She ain't gonna hurt you if you do what she says." She stuck her tongue out at Luke, but she obeyed, walking slowly behind the Indian woman, who was looking intently at plants growing low to the ground.

It was a beautiful fall day, sunny and warm. Daylily felt stronger, but she didn't want to be there with Betty. She thought Betty was creepy and she still missed Granny. It seemed like Luke and Caswell were just glad to be somewhere where they had food, but she had the misery all inside, deep inside, and she felt it.

"Ah, for your cough," Betty said. She picked three or four large pointed leaves off some plants. She found another plant, and pulled off some more leaves and some large purple flowers with red centers. "Soon you will be well, and then what will you do? I know you thinking about running away," she said, looking more at the plants than at Daylily.

"But you scared to run. And that is a good thing to be scared, because of this war. Not safe out there." She bent over and picked another plant. "And this one," she said, holding it out to the girl, "is for your chest."

"Those nasty drinks ain't making me well!" Daylily burst out all of a sudden.

"So, you have better medicine?" She walked at a faster pace. Daylily was now just barely keeping up with the woman. Betty had pulled up her skirts on one side to make it easier to walk in the woods. Her long gray braids were tied in the back with a piece of washed-out gingham. "So, you have a story to tell me?" she said over her shoulder. Daylily had fallen behind. She was having to run to keep up. Betty kept walking.

"No, I don't because you are walking too fast and you know I can't walk that fast, and if you don't stop, I'll run away from you. I'll just run away and you'll have to find me in the woods! You know I'm sick! You know I can't go that fast! Stop it!"

"Oh, you want me to stop now? You have a story to tell me now, Mouth-Stuck-Together?" Betty's basket swung back and forth on her arm gently.

"No, I just wanna, I just wanna . . . keep up."

"Ok, so we gonna walk together," said Betty slowly. She made her steps smaller.

They walked in silence for a while, Betty stopping to pick some strange green raggedy leaves. She pulled them up with the roots. They found a small patch of late blackberries, and Betty reached under the sun-sprinkled leaves to find the best berries. She held out her hand with two or three blue-black berries in it, and smiled. "Now we have peace, Mouth-Stuck-Together?"

Daylily said, "Thank you," but her mouth was set in a line; she didn't look peaceful, and she didn't smile. She ate the berries, and then her eyes began to get tears in them.

"I ain't sad," Daylily insisted, sounding angry. "I just thought about my granny's blueberry cobbler and I missed her, and I's just wonderin what I's doin here with you! I was wondering was I gonna wander forever in these here woods? I's just wantin real bad to be home, to be home *somewhere*, only I think that ain't ever gon happen again."

Daylily was really crying now. She turned her head to the side and wiped her face with the back of her hand.

Daylily plopped down on the ground under a tree. Her soft, teary voice was hard to hear. "Will you let me go home if I tell you my story?"

"Little Mouth-Stuck-Together, you not my prisoner," said Betty, sitting down beside her. "We are both here because there is war. We both prisoners of the stupid men who fight each other. It ain't safe to go or stay. What happened at your home?"

"Granny." She closed her eyes and put her head on her knees. "My granny dead," Daylily said.

Betty could hardly hear her.

"My granny dead and so is Buttercup and her babies." The tears ran out of her eyes and down her chin onto her knees. She began to sob, and all the days she had lived since that horrible night when the soldiers had changed her life forever came spilling out. And Betty Strong Foot put her arms around Daylily and held on to her while she cried. When it was all out of her and Daylily was finally quiet, the shadows had grown longer and the blackberry bush was in the shade.

Betty fished deep within her pocket and pulled out an apple and a pipe. "See this," she said, holding up the pipe. "This here is a present from my man. He gone too. Lost forever. Sometime I cry, sometime I smoke, sometime I pray. Same thing. People come, people go. People cry. People get happy again. But I know somethin. I know he not so far away we can't talk to each other, forever."

For a long time Betty was quiet, and they just sat side by side, leaning against the tree and listening to the afternoon sounds of birds and small animals that they couldn't see, but heard in the woods. "I'm hungry," Daylily said, breaking the silence.

"I'm hungry who?"

"I'm hungry, Betty Strong Foot."

"Oh, Mouth-Stuck-Together is now Mouth-Open! Ha!" She grinned at Daylily, who couldn't help smiling back as Betty held up a green apple. "Let me see. How much can I get me for this apple?"

Daylily looked at her feet. She shrugged. "I don't have nothin. We need to go," she said. "Luke be worried."

Betty put the apple behind her back. "Now let's see. Maybe I can get me a promise for this apple."

Daylily's eyebrows went up slightly.

"Maybe I can get me a promise that Mouth-Open will talk to her granny every night and say prayers to the Great Spirit for Buttercup and her little ones too. And Mouth-Open will ask the angels to help her."

Daylily reached for the apple.

"And," she said, holding the apple just out of Daylily's reach, "that Mouth-Open will be happy again someday soon. Promise."

"Promise!" said Daylily, smiling ever so slightly and snatching the apple. She ran off ahead of Betty, forgetting she didn't know where to go.

Betty caught up with her, dropping most of the leaves for

tea on the ground and laughing. But she kept going in the direction of her house.

"Wait!" Daylily sang out. "Don't you want the leaves?"

"Don't matter!" Betty called back as she stopped to get her breath and wait for the girl. "You gonna get well now, no matter what kinda tea you drink."

During the next several days, Betty Strong Foot was away from home a lot. Luke told Daylily that he thought Betty was out working spells. He thought so because he heard her singing some strange songs one morning, and they were songs he had never heard and words that didn't make sense to him. Once, at dawn, he peeked through the cabin window and saw her coming through the trees on her way back home. She often left after she thought they were asleep, and she came back before she thought they were awake. Sometimes she'd sleep for about four hours and get up, and then she'd give them their chores to do.

One time she came back with lots of food, dried meat and flour and a bag of sugar and apples. She was wheeling it in her old wheelbarrow. Luke and Caswell saw the letters on the bag—U.S. That meant the United States. Luke knew that much. Caswell said he could recognize his ABCs up to G, but he couldn't read it. Betty Strong Foot said White man's letters did not matter as long as they were not hungry. Daylily didn't say anything, but she looked at the letters a long time. Luke wondered why she was staring like that.

That night they had apple pie. They stuffed themselves so much, they felt silly and laughed at everybody and everything. For the first time, Betty could see that Daylily had dimples because she smiled a genuine smile, and the sparkle in Luke's eyes looked real.

Daylily and Caswell had a secret. Daylily bet Caswell that Luke would eat so much he'd have a stomachache before the night was out. Caswell said, "What you got to put up for a wager?" They were whispering over in the corner, by the fire.

"I got my tobacco can," she said. "What you got?"

He screwed up his mouth. "I got two Confederate buttons. Gold ones too. Found em on the ground when you found that tobacco tin."

"They ain't no gold," she teased him. "And anyway, what I gon do with some buttons?"

"Is too! Is too! They real gold. You'll see!"

"I see y'all," said Luke. "Y'all up to some devilment. I can tell." He faked twisting Caswell's arm. "C'mon, tell!" he said.

Caswell wasn't really hurt. They could tell, but he played along hollering and laughing. "No! It's a secret! Lemme go! Lemme go! I'll never tell! Stop!" In the scuffle they knocked over some kindling Betty had piled up, and made a lot of noise.

"I'll find out," Luke said. "Right now I got to finish this pie. If I don't, y'all scalawags be eating my leftovers." He went back to eat, and Daylily and Caswell doubled over with giggles.

"See," she said, "I don tole you. Les go outside and wait. He gon have some terrible stomachache."

"Good idea," said Betty Strong Foot. "Y'all make too much noise. Go back there where the garden is. I can't think." She picked up her pipe. "I'm gon have a smoke."

• • •

Once they had gone to bed, Luke sat up on the dirt floor, and then rolled sideways and groaned. Daylily was about to burst with laughing, but she knew better than to wake Betty Strong Foot, who was snoring.

"Caswell." She shook him. "You wake? Luke got a terrible stomachache, jus like I said. Now you got to give me them buttons."

Caswell turned over and looked at her, and he didn't look happy. His forehead was all wrinkled up in a scowl.

"But I can't," he said. "I can't, Daylily. My papa's a soldier. Maybe those were my papa's. Maybe he lost em. Those buttons . . . maybe . . ."

"It's OK," she said. "Ain't no way I could use real gold buttons anyway." She patted him on the arm. "You sleep tight now." In a few minutes Daylily was asleep.

As the fire died down, Betty roused herself. She got up and checked the children to make sure they were sleeping well. She ate a small piece of leftover pie. Then she dressed and slipped out into the night.

CHAPTER 16

YONA

Once they settled on being there, the days went by one after the other as easy as stringing Betty's beads. Betty taught Daylily how to make a necklace of beads like her own mama had done back in Florida, like the the red and blue one Betty wore every day. Daylily reminded Luke how good it was to have food and a warm place to sleep, and most of all to be with somebody they could depend on. But Luke knew they were not going to stay with Betty forever. He never mentioned it, he just felt it. They had been with Betty for two weeks. Betty said October would be here tomorrow. Caswell had stopped staring at nothing, and Daylily was almost completely well. He couldn't figure it out, but he knew that one day their good time would be over. It just kept bothering him. After a while he pushed it out of his mind altogether. It was too much to worry about.

One night they went into the woods after supper to check the rabbit traps, and there was nothing in them. Betty said she'd have to take the dogs out tomorrow because they needed meat. As they got closer to their cabin, it began to rain. Betty said, "Stay put" and the dogs settled in as Betty tied them to their post in the lean-to.

By the time they reached the door of the cabin, it was raining hard, and there was a chill in the air. Betty restarted the fire so they could all get dry. She made them wrap up in quilts and blankets and made some chicory coffee. She put the pot right on the hot coals so it would boil. Luke could smell the wet leaves and mud all mixed up with the smell of chicory. But he liked it. It smelled like home to him now.

After tussling around about who was gonna sit closest to the fire, they got settled and quiet. Betty's hair was wet from the rain, so she took her hair down and let it hang out so it would dry. Luke noticed her hair was grayer when she took it down. He wondered how old she really was. She said nothing for a long while.

The fire and the rain made the only noise until Caswell said, "Miz Bet—"

"I know what you gonna ask, and it's comin. We goin to the dream lodge. That's what my papa would say when he told me stories. We goin to the dream lodge."

They all squirmed around to get into the most comfortable position.

"That's where the bear lives," Betty said. "Old Mother Bear live in caves in the winter. That's her dream lodge. She knows where to go to be safe. When the wind whistles and shakes the trees, and the rain blows cold, and the snow comes and covers the grass, the water starts to freeze, and she knows she gotta go to the cave to have her babies until it's safe to come out.

"I need to start at the beginning. A long time ago in the old time, it was a cold, cold day. Mother Bear Yona was fishin for dinner. She had to eat a whole lot so she could nurse her babies when they come. She had to eat most everything in sight, and get ready for the cold time. She needed berries and fish. She fished all day and she'd sleep at night.

"Finally she get fat enough. One real cold day, Yona saw a snowflake drop, and then another and then another. Soon the whole world be white, and the snow be thick and deep. Yona knew it was time to go to the dream lodge and sleep for the winter. Under the great mountain, she found a cave just right, and deep inside was a place for her to have her babies and take care of them until spring.

"So the babies come, and Yona nurses the babies, and then one day after a long, long winter in the cave they are ready to go outside. When she gets to the opening of the cave, she is very surprised, for there all by himself is a little boy standin in the shadows. He is scared when he sees Yona, and she asks him to stop cryin. She say, 'Why you cryin, little boy?'

"'Because I am afraid of you, and because my steppapa left me here to starve,' he said. Now this is very strange to Yona. She would never leave her baby bears to starve.

"'Why he leave you?' she say.

"'Because I have seven sisters and brothers and my papa can't feed us all.'

"Yona saw the little boy was startin to cry again. 'Do not worry,' she say. 'I gonna be your mother. You have a name?' Because he did not answer her, she said, 'I will call you Nokosi.'

"All spring Nokosi slept in the cave with his bear mother Yona and his little bear brothers and sister. He thought of them as his own family. They played together and ate lots of fish and berries. Sometimes they had honey when Yona found a nest of bees.

"A whole year went by and Nokosi made friends with all the animals, the wolf, the eagle, the squirrel and the deer. Yona made blueberry cakes for Nokosi and his sister and his two brothers. He was very happy and he loved his bear family.

"But sometimes bad things happen in life, and one day something bad happened in the woods. This one day, Nokosi heard a sound in the woods he had never heard before. Suddenly, he heard his mother bear crashing through the trees.

"'I heard a gun!' she cried. 'Run! Run as fast as you can to our cave! They are hunters! Go! Go fast, and do not stop!'

"Nokosi and his bear family ran as fast as they could to the cave opening. Mother Bear was the last one to enter the cave. She heard the men coming closer and closer, for they wore boots, not moccasins, and they did not know how to run fast and be silent. There were many bear hunters, and Yona knew they could not run fast enough to escape.

"Sometimes there is no way for things to be happy, but the Great Spirit will tell you what is best for you to do if you listen.

"Yona knew how she could save her children, so she whispered to them in the cave, 'I will go out to the men and make a big noise. When I do this, you must run out of the cave and hide. They will not see you, for they will be busy with me.'

"Just as Yona thought, the men did not see her children, because they were too busy shooting at her and trying to kill her with their guns.

"As his mother fell dead, Nokosi stepped out of the trees with the smallest bear, his little bear sister. Her name was Echo.

"'Please do not kill my little sister Echo,' he said. 'You have killed our mother, but we can do nothing to harm you.'

"The men were so amazed to see a human boy that they spared him and his bear sister Echo. Then Nokosi cried over Yona's body and he thanked her spirit for saving him and her other children. He promised he would never kill a mother bear when he grew up, for she had saved him from starving, and she had saved his life. And so he never did.

"The hunters remembered how brave the mother bear Yona was, and they sang praises to her forever. Until the end of their time, the whole village never killed another mother bear."

Luke, Daylily and Caswell were very quiet. They all knew what it was like to lose your mother.

Daylily broke the silence. "But Betty, who looked after Nokosi until he was growed?" she asked.

"Well, his mean stepfather was punished for leavin Nokosi to starve. His mama was long dead, and his older sister looked after him until he was finished growin up. So you see, if you trust Great Spirit, He will always make sure you have somebody carin for you and you ain't never alone. His angels are with you all the time. You might not can see them, but they with you all the time. But you gotta do your job too. You gotta be carin for your brothers and sisters and your animal brothers and sisters, just like Nokosi."

The fire burned slow, and it was close to bedtime.

"You carin for us, Betty," said Daylily, "but who's carin for you?"

"Betty Strong Foot carin for Betty Strong Foot along with a whole passel of angels and spirit animals."

Caswell's eyes opened wide when she said "animals." "Can you tell us about the animals, Betty?"

"Another time I will. Time now for sleepin." She stood up. "Still rainin," she said, and they knew she was not in the dream lodge any more. Suddenly she wrinkled her forehead. Daylily noticed the change on her face.

"What's the matter, Betty?"

"Nothin, thought I heard something. Just the wind and rain, I reckon. C'mon, you young'uns, y'all need to get to bed." As they all got bedded down, the rain kept up even louder on the tin roof, and they all fell asleep to the dance and drumbeat of the rain.

CHAPTER 17

MYSTERIES

Morning brought sunshine and an end to the rain, but it brought a shadow into their lives. Yaller Feet and Pretty Boy, the dogs, had disappeared into the rainy night. Betty went out to take them some fresh water, when she realized how quiet it was. She went to the lean-to shelter where the dogs slept, and there was no sign of them. Since the children had been with her, she had put the dogs out into the little lean-to her papa's dog used to stay in. She had never used it for dogs, only for storage. So she cleaned it out and let the dogs sleep there out of the rain, that is until this morning when they weren't there.

Luke was just stirring when she went back into the cabin. He was sitting up, rubbing his eyes. Betty looked at him. "Don't wake the others yet," she said. "I got something to tell you. Come over here and sit at the table."

Luke rubbed his eyes. He could tell something was wrong.

"You know, Luke, in wartimes folks do crazy things."

Luke looked at Betty, wishing she'd just tell him whatever it was.

"Well, the dogs gone from the lean-to, and I afraid they been stolen."

"But Miz Betty, you think maybe they just run away?" Luke got up and pulled on his jacket that Betty had made him. It was a chilly morning. They were both whispering so as not to wake the others.

"No, Luke, I heard something last night. And remember, I tied them up. I could kick myself!" she hissed. "I should have checked," she said, putting another log on the fire.

"But they was our good *hunting* dogs," said Luke, "and good friends too!"

Betty didn't have the heart to answer him. As she put the kettle on the fire, she said, "Wake the young ones. They have to know."

Luke shook Daylily's shoulder gently. 'Wake up," he said. "We got something to tell you and Caswell. The dogs gone. Maybe stolen."

"What you mean stolen?" she cried. "Who stole them?"

"How do *we* know?" Luke retorted.

This woke Caswell up. "What's wrong, Luke?" he said, rubbing the sleep out of his eyes.

"The dogs," explained Luke. "Some thief took our dogs!"

Caswell was alarmed. "We gotta go find them then!"

"They stole!" Luke and Daylily said together.

Caswell began to cry and then Daylily's eyes filled up with tears. Betty put her arms around both of them.

"Now stop your cryin," she said. "We got food and each other. That's a heap more'n most folks got durin wartimes." Then she got busy trying to get their breakfast together. "Who knows," she said, slamming down a pot for their morning mush. "Maybe they find their way home. Time for breakfast now. Day's a-wastin.'"

Luke counted five days that Betty did not go out at night. He knew because he always woke up when she left. The sixth night she went out and returned just before dawn. Luke heard a whinny just before the door opened. Betty don't have no horse, he thought.

Before he could get scared, she brought in two boxes one at a time, struggling. They must weigh a lot, Luke thought. He had to lie very still to keep her from knowing she was being watched. He could have sworn he heard wagon wheels moving. There was almost no room now in the cabin with the four of them sleeping there, so it wasn't hard for him to see even in the shadows of first light where she stacked the boxes and covered them with a quilt. Luke decided then and there that he'd get into those boxes the next time she went out at night.

He didn't get a chance for another two days. Betty woke him up, stirring around the cabin. He knew it was far into the night. The fire was low. He lay very still and thought maybe she was going outside to pee. Daylily turned over, sound asleep. She was right next to him on their pallet. Betty hesitated as if she was afraid she'd made too much noise. Luke didn't dare move. He opened his eyes just a crack. Over the little lump that Daylily made, he could see Betty in the orange glow, and his breathing almost stopped. She was dressed in a uniform, a rebel uniform, with pants and boots, and she was carrying a rifle! As he watched her, she wound her hair around her head and pulled a large hat down around her face.

Then she blew out the lamp, tiptoed out silently and pulled the door shut behind her.

Luke didn't take a deep breath until he thought she had to be far away. He was listening so hard, he could hear the leaves rustling in the breeze. He heard the logs shifting and sputter-ing in the fireplace, and then he eased himself up, trying not to wake Caswell and Daylily.

He would need some light. The oil lamp was on the table. He turned the wick low and lit it with a piece of twig from the pile that he had to stick into the fire. The boxes were in the dark corner opposite the fireplace and next to the big loom. Luke pulled off the heavy quilt. He kneeled down in order to see better. When he realized he'd never get them open, his heart sank. He needed a crowbar.

Then he looked again, and saw she'd opened one of them herself. A wooden slat had been pried loose. Luke pulled the loose piece of wood as far back as he could, and stuck his hand inside the box. First he felt sawdust. And then he felt the unmistakable barrel of a rifle. The long cold steel, the trigger, he knew too well what it was. Luke stayed on his knees.

Oh, Lordy, now that he knew what was in the boxes, what did it all mean? The rifles, the rebel uniform, her sneaking out in the middle of the night? These boxes didn't say "U.S.," they said something else, a longer word. He couldn't begin to guess what that meant.

A bird called out in the night. Something rustled in the leaves near the side of the house. He blew the lantern out quickly and threw the quilt over the boxes and got very still. Nothing happened. It must have been some kind of animal, he thought. Luke hurried across the dark room and slid into his spot without disturbing his friends, confused and unhappy about what he had seen, but not a minute too soon. As soon as he pulled up the covers, Betty opened the door. For a long time he was afraid to move. He tried breathing like he was asleep. He had that feeling that scared him. A feeling they would have to leave Betty soon. In a few minutes he was asleep.

CHAPTER 18

SECRETS

We have to know what them bags and boxes say!" Luke whispered to Daylily. They were outside, gathering wood for Betty's fire. It had been two more days before he had a chance to tell her what he had seen, and they were both scared.

Daylily especially looked distracted. "I don't want to know," she said, thinking of all the warm meals and the safety of Betty's house. "She ain't bad, you know. She just strange. She treat us real good. Real good. Let's just stay, Luke. Where we gon go anyway? We don't even know where we is! We get out there and get killed by some of them soldiers for sho!"

Luke shook his head. "You a stubborn gal. You know what? It can't be OK to be sneakin around dressed like a man and havin boxes of rifles in the cabin. It ain't right! What she need with all them guns? Maybe one or two, but all them boxes? And a woman supposed to wear skirts! And we gon be in trouble sho nuff if we stays here much longer. Somebody gon come lookin for her and find us. She stealin, that's what I think. You know what they do to niggers what steal! And we gon be hauled up fore the White man and be strung up for stealin!" A breeze ruffled leaves over their heads.

Daylily looked up at the sky. "Luke, the trees have started losing their leaves. We can't go now. How about if we leave in the spring? What we gon do? Caswell get cold in the woods, and maybe sick like I did? He too little."

She shivered even though Betty had given her a heavy shirt to wear. All three of them were dressed in the gray and blue clothes she made out of old uniforms that Betty said someone gave her.

Caswell was about twenty feet away, making popping noises with a stick rifle, playing soldier. His hair had grown a lot. He ran in and out of the cabin every few minutes, said something to Betty about his game and ran back out again. Betty had tied his hair back Indian-style. She had laughed and laughed at Luke, whose black, curly hair was wild and uncontrollable, and standing all over his head now. But it was clean, at least. She made them wash themselves regularly.

"Did you see her this morning?" said Luke, looking back to make sure Betty was still in the house. "She was all scratched up. Look like she'd been in a scrap, and she don't look good, like she been hurtin. Somethin happened, I tell you, and she almost got caught stealin. That's what I believe, and I say we should light out."

"Shh," Daylily whispered. "She comin out the door. I got somethin to tell you. I'll tell it later."

They didn't have another chance to talk until late that night while Betty was gone. They were both restless and waiting for her to change clothes and leave. Only she didn't dress up. She just left in her own clothes with a basket on her arm. It was close to dawn when she silently opened the door and left.

The basket had a loaf of light bread, or something in it that was soft. Daylily was sure of that. She had peeked with one eye and saw her covering it with a napkin.

Luke wanted to look at the rifles again. He was rarin to show Daylily what he'd found.

When they leaned over the boxes in the corner, Daylily told him, "I got to tell you somethin, Luke."

"What? Hurry up! She might come back. Lemme show you what I found!"

"No, wait! I gotta tell you," she whispered. "I knows what these words are. I can read. I reckon it's safe to tell you now."

"What? This ain't no time to be funnin me, gal. You can't read. You tellin a big ole lie. This here's important, and we got to figure out what to do."

"Naw, I ain't, Luke. I ain't funnin you. Look-a here. This say 'U.S.' and this say 'Union Pro-vi-si-on.'" Luke's mouth stood open while he realized what this could mean.

"How you get learnin?" he asked her.

"Granny. She knowed how, and she learnt me," she explained, a sly smile on her round face.

"What's that pro-vi-si-on?" Luke asked. Daylily shrugged. "And look-a here," he said, his whisper careless and loud. "What's this mean? This long one?"

"Con-fed-er . . ."

"—ate!" Luke finished the word he had heard so many times. "The rebs! She stole them from the rebs!"

Too late to move a muscle, they were both aware of someone standing right behind them. They heard Betty's low and very calm voice, speaking a language they didn't understand. And then she said, "Betty Strong Foot is not a thief. But you, you steal something from me cause you put your nose where it does not belong. Would you like to know what happens to the noses of thieves?"

CHAPTER 19

CAUGHT

Daylily and Luke were too scared to answer as she grabbed both their noses and dragged them into the middle of the floor. They each gasped for breath. "Betty Strong Foot works for food. She has never been a thief!" She shook them by the nose and let them go so suddenly, they lost their balance and fell down. "You want to know what I do? I am a spy! I am spy for the stupid men who killed my man. I carry secrets for the Union, and I carry secrets for the rebels because I hate them both, because they kill and they are too stupid to catch me! And now you know what you should not know. Now you must stay with Betty. If you get caught, you get scared, and you tell. You stay till the war is over. I am not happy, you know. Now, get the little one up. You go and wash. Bah! It's over. Get up, time we all eat. It's morning now."

It was a long day. Luke and Daylily were now afraid to make Betty mad, and they could only make signs to each other when she was in the cabin. Daylily spent all day rubbing her sore nose, and wondering what secrets Betty carried, and what *pro·vi·si·ons* meant. A couple of times Luke tried to think how he could say he was sorry. Only Caswell seemed to be content.

Luke knew a little about what spies did. There had been talk on Massa Higsaw's place about spies. He knew they were shot or strung up if they got caught, that he was sure of.

What did she mean, she hated them both? Luke asked himself. The South and the North? How could she say that? Everybody was on either one side or the other. The South hated the North, even though they were both White. The North hated the South because the rebs was against President Lincoln. And the rebs hated colored folks worse'n anybody at all, and didn't want colored to be free.

Was Betty Strong Foot for colored or White? Luke wanted to ask her but he didn't dare. She said she was free. She said her Daddy was colored, and she had White folks hair, but that didn't mean nothin cause so did Pecola back home, and she sure was one of Massa Higsaw's niggers same as he was. She said her mama was Indian. Betty's skin was as dark as his almost.

He knew one thing though, spying sure wasn't safe, and if she was in danger, they were in danger. Still it was good being with her and like Daylily said, they knew right enough what danger was out there on the road. He thought about the field full of dead bodies, and Daylily almost dying and the mountain lion, and being hungry enough to steal, and soon Luke convinced himself that they should stay put. She was real good to them. They had hot meals and even treats once in a while, and they all felt like family.

CHAPTER 20

LITTLE BEAR

It was a warm afternoon, even for early November. Locusts were crying. But the smell of fall hit them as they stepped out into the yard. With their stomachs full of Betty's biscuits and molasses they had plenty of energy to play until the darkness hit. They had been at work all day.

"First we clean the cabin," Betty had told them, "then we weed. Then maybe we eat something, if you good."

"You not gonna feed us if we not good?" said Caswell, looking very worried and wrinkling up his nose.

Betty kept her face very straight. "Nope."

Luke grinned at Daylily and they all laughed at Caswell's face. They had to get the garden weeded. She had to set out sweet potatoes and they had to help. Only Caswell didn't know how to work, because he had never worked a day in his life.

"Boy, you don't know nothing," said Luke. "You ain't never lifted a finger!"

"Have too," said Caswell, only he couldn't think of anything he knew how to do. Betty said to quit fussin; they had to weed lima beans and late squash all afternoon, so they were more than ready for an all-out romp when they finished. It had been a day when none of them thought much about what to-morrow might bring, or what yesterday had done.

It had been a day when Daylily didn't think about But-tercup, not one time. A day after a night when the bad dream didn't come.

One bad morning Betty looked her real hard in the face and said, "Come with me, we gotta talk," and they walked around the cabin not too far away, but too far away for the boys to hear what they were really saying.

She asked Daylily to tell her what was in the dream, and Daylily told her how she thought her hands was cut off.

Betty said, "Come on now, you know what you gonna do."

Daylily said, "We gonna ask the angels to take it . . ."

"Take it away," Betty said for her, "cause it happened in the past and it's gone away and it ain't coming back."

Once Daylily asked, "Are the angels Black?"

"The Great Spirit don't care if they Black, White or Red, or they got no color. They still angels. Just like you can call Him Great Spirit or God, and He don't care bout that," Betty said. "Just like these trees and flowers, all of em be angels."

The next time she dreamed, she told Betty about it.

"The angels had Black faces" she said, "and they wore long blue dresses. That's the color I like best."

But last night the dream didn't come, and today she was thinking only about what Betty might have for supper, and finding some blue wildflowers to put on the table in a cup, and how pretty that would look, blue cornflowers, false pen-nyroyal, and chicory. So she asked Betty if she could go looking for flowers.

Betty said, "Ok, only don't be gone so long."

"Y'all hide, and I'll be it," Luke said, ready to take the lead as usual.

Daylily didn't even care that he had beat her to it. She didn't really want to play. She was off to find flowers and be alone. These days, she felt free like the birds, like the chicka-dee with the black cap of feathers on its head, like the mock-ingbird. Sometimes it felt so good it was scary to her. Nobody was coming to tell you to pick crops faster. Nobody was crying about hurting arms and legs. Nobody dying and nobody being sold away.

It was kind of nice being in the quiet by herself. She was never left by herself here at Betty's, and she never remembered being by herself back at home. She was always with Granny or with the pickers.

She found some spiderwort and remembered that Betty had made her some tea out of that when she had a stomachache. She would put the blue flowers on the table and they would thank the Great Spirit, cause Betty would make them, and they would eat molasses and biscuits and salt pork and butter beans. She wandered a little farther, farther than she would have if she had been worried about her dream that day.

When she looked up, there were lots of pine trees, more trees than she remembered seeing around Betty's house, and there were lots of tangled vines and one or two big tree branches that had fallen during a storm. She was farther away than she had ever been from the cabin. She thought maybe she should go back, but she could see the sky through the treetops and it was still almost blue violet. She didn't hear the river that ran be-hind Betty's house, and she didn't hear the boys any more.

Then she saw a whole bunch of bellflowers up ahead. Betty

used them for coughs. The first time she'd had some was when she was getting over the sickness she got in the woods. She looked around to see if there were any bellflowers closer to her, and then she noticed something strange.

A half-smoked cigarette. Right by her feet. Not Betty's, she knew. Betty only smoked a pipe. Whose was it if it wasn't Betty's? And where was the person who had smoked it? All at once the woods seemed to get very quiet. Daylily felt a chill, a chill that reminded her of something she didn't want to re-member ever again. She didn't want to think about the bad stuff, but she remembered it all. It just kept coming at her. She was staring at the soggy cigarette, like somebody'd put her in a spell.

And then she noticed next to an oak tree what looked like the print of somebody's foot in the damp mud. She was still standing in the same place and the flowers were up ahead. It seemed to get very dark there in the trees. She raised her head, and on the other side of the flowers was something that looked like an old campfire that had been put out by the rain. There was something not right about that. A person had been there, maybe a long time ago, maybe not. She saw an old tin cup on the ground, but what she didn't see was someone standing in the shadows.

In the stillness of the woods, there was a small sound. She started. A familiar sound. The sound of a dog whining, no, the sound of a dog almost crying, crying like a baby, like he might be hurt or sick. She felt like she was fastened to the ground, too scared to move. She thought about how upset Betty had been last month when the dogs disappeared, and when she thought that, it was the first time she had the sense to move at all, but she was afraid to stay and afraid to go.

The breeze ruffled her cotton skirt. Brown leaves rustled in the slight wind. Goose bumps rose on her arms as she thought about leaving the dog to die, and then the dream came into her head, just like it had never left, and she was back in the woods alone just like before. The men and the screams and the knife and the babies, and the whimpering of Buttercup as she died.

Daylily sagged under the weight of her memory and found herself on her knees, weeping and shaking. She was so scared and so alone. She thought she was going to die in the woods, and she remembered Betty saying what we gonna do with that dream when it come, what we gonna do . . . ask the angels to take it away . . . take it away.

Little by little she could hear herself breathe again, and she stopped the terrible shaking, and she heard the dog again. She knew she couldn't leave him out there to die all by himself, and she came back to her self and felt her body touching the ground. She felt the leaves and the mud and the twigs on the ground under her arms and legs.

She had to take him back home or she had to sit with him while he died. There was nobody to sit with Buttercup while she died cause Daylily was hiding, and nobody to sit with Daylily while she was so scared and alone. No, she didn't care if that ole man came back, whoever he was. Maybe this was one of Betty's dogs, maybe he ran away from whoever took him. Maybe he was really hurt, maybe even dying. She couldn't let the bad stuff come back into her head.

The dog must have sensed someone was near. He whined even louder. She just had to see if it was Yaller Feet or Pretty Boy. It sounded like he was hurting really bad.

Daylily stood up and put one foot in front of the other slowly, quietly. The closer she got to the sound, the more she was sure it was Yaller Feet. "Yaller Feet," she whispered. "That you?" Then as she looked to her left, she thought she saw a shadow. It was one of those fallen logs, and on the other side of the log was the dog. Yaller Feet was lying on his side. A dirty, old frayed rope was tied around his neck. He was too hurt even to wag his tail at her, but she thought she saw his eyes telling her that he was glad to see somebody from home.

He had been beat up really bad by somebody and looked like he had torn the rope and run away. His face was bloody and his side was cut bad. He whined softly and closed his eyes. The bones in his side kind of poked out from his skin. She wanted to cry. Who would do this awful thing to him? Whoever he had been with, they had hardly fed him for the three weeks he'd been gone. The man with the cigarette, she was sure.

Nobody had been here in a while, though. She felt the fire and the ashes were stone cold. She had to get back. It was beginning to get darker, and she had to find her way. And she would have to carry Yaller Feet.

All she had with her were her flowers that she had dropped on the other side of the log, nothing to help carry the dog. She looked around in the twilight. She saw where a piece of log had rotted and broken off. It was almost as long as the dog. If she could drag it over to Yaller Feet and pick him up or put him on it, she could push him back home. He needed water. She knew that. Without it he would die soon.

His bloody face was dry. It looked like more than one day since someone had beat him and left him for dead, and he had tried to get all the way back home.

Daylily pulled the wooden shell of a log over to the wounded dog. He was too weak to growl when she picked him up, but he yelped in pain. She didn't have far to lift him, and that was good because he was not a little dog. Then she had to push him or pull him all the way back to the cabin, and which way was that? She remembered where she saw the blue flowers. She took a big breath and started off pulling. The dog was heavy. Almost a dead weight. Grunting, puffing and blowing, she said out loud, "Don't you die on me, you Yaller Feet dog, don't you die on me." She heard Betty's voice in her head saying, "There's always someone carin for you, a whole passel of angels and spirit animals." Lord, Daylily thought, I need them angels, now, Lord. Tell me which way to go. Guide my feet, Lord.

It was almost dark. She had gone maybe forty feet. He was still alive. Her legs were scratched up from brambles and twigs, and her hands were really sore when she heard the river water, and then she knew they were somewhere near the house. It's not too long now, she thought.

"Just you hang on, Yaller Feet," she said in a whisper. "We almost there. Just please hang on."

When she bent over to start pulling the hollow log again, she saw two well-worn moccasins out of the corner of her eyes.

She almost jumped out of her skin until she recognized Betty's legs and looked up into three worried faces.

"Little Bear," said Betty, "you are some kinda fierce mama bear. Next time you run off to save a dog, tell somebody. You had us worried almost to death! Luke, run get me a quilt. Let's see can we save Yaller Feet here!"

CHAPTER 21

DISGUISE

One late November day, Betty told them she had a mission to carry out. Luke's heart tightened. It made him scared to think of her doing these dangerous things. If she'd just leave it alone, he thought. Just let it be.

But she had a plan. It was true she had almost been captured on that October night she came back scratched up. Now she needed another disguise and another plan that would be almost foolproof. She said she had people depending on her messages and couldn't let them down.

They weren't looking for a woman with a child, she told Luke. There were so many people wandering around looking for food, they could be just another hungry mother and child, and if something happened and she was caught, well, Caswell was an orphan, like as not, and one of their own. They'd probably put him in a home for orphans. If they didn't get back by sundown, Daylily and Luke should strike out for the North. Harper's Ferry was not too far up the road.

So the next morning, while Luke was finishing his cornmeal patty, Betty was explaining the plan to Caswell. "We going on a great adventure, and leave the big ones at home. We going to meet some friends of mine, just the two of us." She made up a bundle with tobacco and gunpowder, dried fish, and one gold coin, tied it in a piece of homespun cloth and gave it to Luke.

Caswell was excited. He babbled on about how he had to be in disguise so the Yankees wouldn't snatch him if they were in the woods, and how his daddy would be proud of him.

Luke didn't much like to think of Betty helping Caswell's daddy, but he didn't say so, knowing it would hurt Caswell's feelings. He remembered the field of dead soldiers he had seen, and thought to himself, He just don't know how scary this gon be.

Daylily and Luke watched while Betty worked on the disguise. She made a mixture of red clay and coffee and then painted it on Caswell's skin with a piece of cloth.

"His face look dirty," said Daylily.

Betty nodded. "That's OK. Poor folks get dirty. Nobody have time to haul water during war." She daubed some of it onto his hair, and combed it through, then tied it back with a leather thong. "Give me that cap, Luke."

"You right sure this gonna work?" said Luke, handing her the hat.

"Luke," she said, looking at the older boy's worried eyes, "we need supplies for food. We need supplies for the winter. Starvin to death is worse than bein shot." She pulled the hat down low over Caswell's forehead.

"This is the way Betty Strong Foot get supplies. For four people, need more supplies than for one. Yes? Caswell and Betty have to work." Then she pulled a shawl around her face. "Back soon. You'll see."

She bundled Caswell in a shirt and a little jacket she had

made for him. She took his hand. Luke watched as the late morning sun started on its daily journey while they walked into the woods. The river water shone in the November sun.

Daylily stood with him and watched them disappear. They went into the cabin and sat down in front of the fire. Neither one of them spoke a word. Finally, Daylily broke the silence. "Guess we better do our chores, Luke."

"Guess so," he answered. "It something to do anyway." Luke's job was to see that the woodpile didn't get down too low. He wasn't too good yet with the saw, so he got smaller branches. Daylily was supposed to cut up apples for the drying rack, and they were both supposed to weed the winter garden where their winter vegetables were planted.

They worked very slowly. The day seemed to drag on and on. To pass the time Daylily worked on some doll clothes she was making.

Betty had left them some midday dinner, squirrel stew and biscuits. They ate quietly, each one feeling the other's mood.

"I can't stand this quiet," Daylily said. "Why you so sad? They comin back. Ain't she always come back before? Why she ain't comin back this time? You look like death done come in the house, Luke."

He shook himself. He didn't want her to know he was scared. "So what we gon talk about? You don tole me all the stories you got to tell, and I reckon I done the same. Let's play blind man's bluff."

After blind man's bluff in the house, they played hide-and-seek outdoors until it was almost dark and they had run out of places to hide. Night came on early in November. They didn't want to get too far away from the cabin or from each other.

They played guessing games until they were exhausted and the darkness had caught them. The fire had almost burned out in the cabin, and they were getting sleepy.

"Got to feed the dog," said Luke, realizing it was getting late. He took some dried meat Betty had kept for the dog and went outside. "Here, Yaller Feet," he said. His voice was low and small. "Here, boy." Yaller Feet got up slowly. He was still healing up from his ordeal. Betty had been tying him up in front of the house since the thief took him. When Luke saw the dog at the edge of the clearing that was Betty's garden, he threw the meat down and went back inside.

"Must be past Caswell's bedtime," Daylily said as Luke came through the door.

"Should be back by now," said Luke almost in a whisper.

"First time we ain't been together since . . . you know . . . that night." Daylily frowned.

"Yeah, sho is."

"Can't do nothin bout it though . . . I don't feel so good, Luke."

"Lie down. Rest yourself. You don't wanna get poorly again."

"Where she go, you think?" Daylily stretched out on her pallet.

Luke threw a sharp look at Daylily. "You ain't thinking she got caught . . . ?"

"Naw, just wonderin where'd she go. Ain't no towns around here. Nothin but the river and the trees. Don't know where that Harper's Ferry place is she talks about."

"Where there's a river, there's a town," Luke said. "Always like that sooner or later. Harper's Ferry on the Shenandoah, Betty said."

He wanted to sit up, stay awake, and watch for Betty and Caswell, but he kept nodding off, so he built the fire for the night and ate a piece of corn bread he found, fussing around the cabin, just keeping himself busy. What if she had turned Caswell over to the rebel soldiers? They'd come and find the rest of them, that's what. And he and Daylily would be put in jail or worse, or so he thought.

By the time they reached the farmhouse, it was noon and Caswell was hungry. They stood in front of a very small run-down house. It needed painting, there was no glass in the one window, and the door was hanging half off. Caswell thought it looked like nobody had lived there for a long, long time.

Betty said, "That's the house, Caswell. You just stand next to me and be quiet." She stood outside the door and gave three knocks. Then she said, "Gather roun the flag, boys."

When the door opened, a tall dirty White man stood there. His clothes were torn, and he had a beard. He smelled bad, like whiskey. The whole place smelled like strong drink.

Betty said, "Is this the house of Master Jones?"

The dirty man said, "Who's askin?"

And then two other men came to the door, and Betty said to the first one, "Mister, we lost." Caswell didn't know why Betty had said that since she had just said this was the house. Before he could even think about it, the three men grabbed Betty, and he started screaming.

"We know you the Indian what's been spyin on us!"

Betty's face horrified Caswell. He'd never seen her look like that. She yelled in a rough voice, "You got the wrong Indian! Don't you see I got my boy?" Then she yelled, "Run! Caswell, run! Go home!" But he was riveted to the floor with fear. The three men were trying to hold Betty. But they couldn't hold her. They hit her. She fought, and one of them lunged for him so fast, he was caught. He saw Betty pull a knife from under her blouse and stab the man who had grabbed him. The man fell forward, choking. A chair hit the wall and splintered. Blood went everywhere. The whole place was noise and confusion.

"Run!" Betty screamed at Caswell. "Run!"

The men were yelling curses.

Caswell ran out in the yard looking for someplace to hide. The first thing he saw was a horse and wagon, but he was too short to get into it. He struggled to get into the wagon for a few crazy seconds, and then he saw some big hay bales and got behind them. He heard groans and yells coming from the house. He heard the stabbed man hollering, "Help me! I'm bleedin bad! I'm dyin. Help!"

One said, "The boy! Where is he?"

And another said, "Leave him! He don't matter!"

Just then, Caswell peeked from behind the hay bale, and he saw the two men and Betty fall out the front door into the yard. The two men were knocking Betty around. She fought back, kicking one man in the shins and trying to use her knife. She cut one of the men in the face and arm.

"Damn," he swore. "Get her! Get her!" and finally he knocked her down and took her knife, and she stayed down. Then they got a rope and tied her up. "We gonna kill you, squaw," one said. "But first we gotta git some help for Joe, and then we gonna find out what you know. Just you sit here and think about *how* we gonna make you talk!"

Betty spit at the man.

He slapped her face so hard, it made her head bounce. Caswell was having trouble breathing. His chest felt like it was tied with ropes. His legs were quivering. As the two men dragged Betty to a shed that was on the place, Caswell took off, running for his life, headed toward Betty's cabin.

CHAPTER 22

FAMILY

Some katydids whined in the night. Luke could hear the lap-lap sounds of the river, it was so quiet. He was just about to give up and lie down when he heard something or someone outside. He stood very still. If it wasn't Betty and Caswell, he'd be ready for whoever it was. The rustle of leaves came closer. It sounded small, not heavy. He thought it was some kind of animal. Luke brought his breath in sharply. "Daylily, you hear that?"

She sat up, awake all at once.

Oh, Lordy, don't let it be another mountain lion, Luke thought. Then someone knocked on the door and they heard Caswell. "Luke, Luke, Daylily, it's me! Open the door. It's me! It's me!" Caswell pummeled the door with his small fists.

Luke took the bar off the door and Caswell threw his arms around Luke's waist.

"They took her," he cried, sobbing now that he was safe, "and put her in a shed. And they might shoot her, or hang her, or they might put her in jail. Oh, Luke, what's gonna happen to us?"

"Slow down a minute, whoa! Hold your horses! Caswell!

Caswell!" Luke grabbed hold of Caswell's arm and took a good look at his face. Between the tears and the makeup Betty had put on him, he looked like he had stripes. His hair had long since come out of the leather thong Betty had tied around it, and he was a wild sight. His legs and arms were scratched by bushes and red from insect bites, and his trousers were torn. Altogether he looked like he had come through a war all by himself.

"Hush now, boy, tell me what you sayin about Betty. Slow down. Slow down! Stop cryin and tell us." Luke had heard enough to dread what was coming.

Caswell took a deep, ragged breath.

"Daylily, give him a drink so's he can talk," Luke said. Daylily had been standing there all along, struck speechless by the confusion.

Caswell gulped down some water. "We went to a farmhouse over yonder. We walked a long time, and Betty told me that if we got separated, I should follow the river road back here to you and Daylily." He talked in a strange, squeaking voice, and he was still shaking, but he told Luke and Daylily the whole story. "I cut out fast comin back here, and they must not have seen where I was cause nobody followed me. But what's gonna happen to us now?" Big tears ran down his streaked face.

Daylily put her arm around him. "Don't you feel bad now, Caswell, you come back to tell us Betty in trouble. You did good!"

"Oh, Lordy," Luke said, "let me think. Let me think."

Daylily's eyes filled up with tears. "I'm thinkin that Betty is dead now," she said. "I can't stand no more dyin."

"Wait, it ain't time for snivelin," Luke said. "Not yet. Us

got to have a plan. Maybe us can find her and set her loose. How far is this place, Caswell?"

"Over yonder" was all he could say.

"Well, wait a minute. Wait. Where was the sun when y'all got to that house? Think hard now. Straight overhead or comin down?"

"I remember, I remember! She said it was getting on to din-nertime. Sun was straight over our heads when we saw the house."

"It's a far piece then," said Luke, "cause y'all left this mornin. OK, we got to sleep now, and rest up. Get a little food together for the trip and rest up. We gots to walk a long way and try to help Betty Strong Foot."

"Luke, I'm scared," said Daylily.

Caswell said, "Me too."

"Me too," said Luke, "but we gotta try. She helped us. She saved our lives. And now it's time for us to help her. We gon start at first light. It's too late now. Don't wanna be out in these woods and run into another mountain lion. We just fol-low the river."

Caswell was glassy eyed and seemed to be far away. "I did it, Luke, didn't I? I walked all the way back, and it got dark and I didn't get lost or nothin. I made it . . . all by myself?"

"You did, Caswell. You sho nuff did!"

Caswell's smile stretched from cheek to cheek.

"Think you can find it again?"

"Sho nuff!" said Caswell, trying to sound like Luke.

This hit a funny bone in Daylily and Luke, and Caswell laughed at his own joke as hard as they did. It was so good not to be crying or worrying for a few minutes that they fell all over each other like ordinary children.

"And go wash your filthy face," said Luke to Caswell. "You are a sight to behold. If you could just see yourself, you be scared sho nuff!" That started the laughter all over again, and they pointed fingers at each other. They laughed at the state of Luke's hair, and Caswell's face with the streaks of makeup and dust. They laughed until their stomachs hurt, until they were finally exhausted. And then a quiet shadow settled on their faces and they gathered in front of the fire.

"We gotta pray now," Daylily said. "We gotta pray Betty be OK, and that we find her and we don't get killed like Buttercup and her babies, and that we all gets back home somewhere safe and sound. Y'all bow your heads," she said.

For once Luke didn't argue with her.

"God," she said, "this here's Daylily callin on You. We down here just little chirren," she said, "cept Luke, who's a little bigger than us. And we scared to death, Lord, and we callin on You in our time of need."

"Amen," said Luke.

"And we just want to ask you, Lord, to bless us and help us find our Betty Strong Foot, cause she sure did save our lives."

"Amen," said Luke.

"And she a good woman, Lord, who in trouble, and Lord, we don't know if You hold with that spy work she doin, Lord, but please don't take it to heart, and keep us safe. Amen."

"And Lord," Luke added, "if You don't like what she doin, please don't take it out on us. Thank you, Jesus. Amen."

Daylily nudged Caswell. "Say amen."

Caswell said, "Amen."

"Everybody lay down and rest," said Luke. In the quiet that followed they could hear each other breathing. Sensitive to each other now, each one knew the others were not asleep.

"Luke," whispered Caswell, "you sleep?"

"Uh unh."

"Luke?"

"What?"

"Can White people be related to Negras?"

"Sometimes they is."

"Luke?"

"What?"

"Can I be your little brother?"

"Yeah."

"Is that wrong?"

"No, but don't tell nobody I say it's OK. We get in trouble."

"OK."

"Night."

"Night."

CHAPTER 23

RESCUE

They got themselves together at dawn, Caswell leading this time. Luke could tell Caswell felt very important in spite of being scared. He marched as far ahead of them as he could. "Don't you be getting so far ahead up there," Luke said to the younger boy. "We needs to stay together."

They had Betty's corn bread, and Daylily had wrapped it in scraps of Betty's gingham. Luke had filled the canteens. Caswell got hungry first, so they stopped to eat.

"Don't eat it all," Luke said. "You be hungry fore we get half there." The birds were singing their hearts out, and when the sun was high, Luke said, "Midday now. And look up ahead there; it's a house!"

"This is it," said Caswell. "This is it!" It was the shabby, unpainted house with the door half off where he and Betty had been before.

"Shh, we can't let nobody hear us," Luke warned. "What if they catch us, and then we as good as cooked!"

"Oh, mercy me," whispered Daylily, "we in trouble for sure!" Somewhere a cat whined. Then they saw her. She was white, gray and starving. Her bones were almost poking through the gray fur. She mewed insistently, wanting to be fed.

"Go way! You makin too much noise!" Daylily whispered. "We ain't got no food for you. You give us away! Go head on!" she whispered again urgently, pushing the cat with her foot.

The meows of the gray cat cut into the air. For a minute Luke's heart failed him. He was sure if anybody was there, they'd come out to see what was wrong with that fool cat, and they would all be shot for being spies, or at least sent back to Massa Higsaw's and Massa Riverson's. But then the cat stopped, and he saw why. Daylily was feeding it her corn bread to keep her quiet.

"This ain't no time to get cold feet," Luke whispered, mostly to himself. "We done decided back at the house. Come on, let's see is she in these sheds over yonder. She could be anywhere. They could have taken her away by now."

It didn't look like there was a soul on the place. It was deathly still. Over near a big tree in a field next to the house was the wagon Caswell had tried to get into, and a horse was hooked up to it. The horse was tied to the tree. Tall yellow grass and lots of weeds grew all around the house.

Caswell was sure he had seen two horses when he arrived with Betty, but there were no other animals in sight. Unless the second one was in the ramshackle barn. There was a path worn from the house to the barn.

Maybe they had already taken Betty and killed her was the thought on all their minds. Somewhere a woodpecker was making a hole in a tree, and locusts buzzed. A creaky sound was coming from one of the small outbuildings like a door loose on its hinges.

"Wait, shh," Luke warned. "What's that?" Then he saw the door moving gently in the breeze. He tiptoed up to the shed and looked in. "Unless they's hidin in the house, don't look like nobody here," he said. "Not a soul. All I saw was lots of spiderwebs."

"But that's where they took her!" Caswell whispered.

"Well, she ain't here no more," said Luke.

Then he really heard something. Someone or something had fallen inside the shack of a house.

Daylily heard it too. She gasped and looked at Luke as if to warn him. They heard a man swear. He sounded angry. But was Betty in there? There was only one thing to do. Someone had to look inside the house. Caswell whispered, "But they took her over there."

"Caswell, hush," Luke said under his breath. "Y'all, if we gets caught, let me do the talking I'll say we was just on our way home, and stopped to see if we could have a drink of water." Luke raised his hand and motioned for the younger ones to stay put. Tiptoeing over to the window, he peeked inside and quickly hunched down, so as not to be seen, moving backward toward Daylily and Caswell.

He shook his head as if to say she wasn't there and pointed toward the other shed. It was about twenty yards away across a clearing.

"Maybe she in that one," whispered Luke. "Come on, y'all." When they started toward the second outbuilding, Luke kept looking back at the house, praying the man inside would stay there. This shed was closed up tight. Unlike the other one, there were no loose doors here, and no windows. Luke got all the way up to the door and stood there, listening.

"Go on, Luke, open it!" Caswell whispered.

"Shh, somethin's in here." Luke put his eye up to a crack in the wall.

"Let me see!" Caswell said. Luke motioned to Caswell to be silent, putting his own finger up to his mouth. "Can't see nothin, too dark. Have to open the door." He cracked the door, poised to run if necessary. And then they all let out a whoop, clapping their hands over their mouths when they remembered they had company. There she was, all tied up. Lying on the floor with a rag in her mouth. Betty's eyes were wide with surprise when she saw them. Luke loosened the gag and Betty couldn't help grinning, even though her mouth was swollen and black and blue.

"Shh, be quiet now," she warned, "and for God's sake, y'all young'uns get me loose!"

Daylily was so glad to see Betty, she almost cried. Caswell was hanging on her neck, and Luke was trying to untie the knots.

"Had me hog-tied!" she whispered, "but you young'uns is here!" Her legs were numb and sore, and she rubbed them fast. "I ain't never been so glad to see somebody in my whole life!"

"Hush, y'all!" warned Luke. "That man gonna hear us!"

"How many of em are in the house, Luke?" Betty loosened the last of the knots herself. She gave them all a hurried hug.

"Just one that I saw, Betty."

"That don mean nothing," she whispered. "Could be more. Drunken trash they was. We got to get out of here."

Betty cracked the door of the shed and motioned silently for them to follow. Just as they got all the way outside, the man in the house came down the steps and into the yard. They all stopped breathing.

But he didn't see them. He was on his way to the outhouse that was on the other side of the shack, and he was fumbling with his overalls. As soon as he had stumbled into the out' house, Betty said, "Get in the wagon yonder, quick!"

Luke lifted Caswell into the wagon, Daylily scrambled on, and Betty got the horse loose. She leapt into the front seat and flicked the reins hard.

"Giddup!" she said sharply, and they took off flying down the road, faster than lightning. Nobody looked back. They all heard him cussing and shouting at them. Luckily he hadn't taken his gun with him to the outhouse.

CHAPTER 24

SMALLPOX

Back on her land, Betty worked quickly. She turned the wagon around and slapped the horse's haunches. He started off down the road as she hoped he would, and she prayed he'd make his way home so they wouldn't come looking for their horse. She had seriously wounded a man, and now she would be called a horse thief, an occupation not too uncommon in the war. If she got caught as a spy now, she'd be hanged for sure. Still she couldn't help smiling. Don't that just beat all, she thought. Caswell got through! She couldn't believe it; she had to laugh. The little pathfinder made his way back!

"I would have been a dead duck!" she said to the children. "Because I was supposed to meet someone else. They were the wrong men."

She couldn't take any chances. She thought about those guns and the other "stolen" goods from Union and Confederate sides both. There was no way she could get rid of the evidence fast enough.

As they approached her house, she motioned to all the children to stay back. No need for all of them to get hurt. "Listen," she whispered, "if anybody in the house, run and hide. Don't try to get help. Betty Strong Foot be OK. Hide till you see them leave, then come home, get food, and go north to Harper's Ferry. Understand? Stay here and watch. Betty Strong Foot be OK."

Luke looked at the others. They didn't ask any questions. They all knew this was serious business.

She picked up the largest stick she could find. She usually wore a knife under her blouse, but they had taken it away after she'd stabbed that man.

She slowly pushed the door with the stick. It opened silently. Once into the cabin, she could see every corner. She checked behind all the big boxes, and anywhere a person could fit. Something was off. There was a jar of her best homemade blackberry wine on the table. And she could smell it—the scent of something foreign invading her space. "Nobody here," she told them, and put her fingers to her mouth to signal that they should be quiet.

She motioned them forward. But she still was not sure it was safe. In some mysterious way, it was too quiet. And strangely, Yaller Feet was not there.

Once they were all in, the children looked at her, puzzled because she was still whispering. "Somebody's been here. Be quiet as a mouse," she said. "I looking outside." The children froze, afraid to stay and afraid to go with her.

Finally, she found it, outside in the back, and she called into the cabin. "Luke, Luke, come out here! Only don't you come too close!" She was nervous, but not frightened.

Luke crept up to her until she motioned to him to stop. A man was on the ground. "He dead?" Luke asked, hardly daring to breathe.

"No, not yet," she said, "but he almost gone. See can you

help me get him turned over." They tugged at the uncon-
scious man, who moaned when they turned him. He was
White, a soldier; she knew that from his hat, or maybe he had
stolen it.

"What ails him, Betty?" Luke asked.

"Don't know. He skin and bones, burnin up with fever. Get
me some cool water, Luke, and a rag. Could be something bad,
could be something not so bad." Looked to be Union, Betty
thought. She checked his pockets and found a dusty letter
with dried blood on it.

"Kin you read, Luke?" Betty was sponging off the man's
face with an old rag Luke had found inside. Daylily and Caswell were standing in the cabin too scared to ask what had
happened and afraid to call out loud.

"No, ma'am, that's a fact . . . but . . . I guess I can tell it
now. Daylily can read some.

"Lookee here, y'all," called Luke, running into the cabin.
"Come see. A soldier most dead and a letter. Miz Betty want
you to read this letter to her, Daylily."

Caswell and Daylily hurried up to Betty. "You don't mind
I kin read?" said Daylily.

"Why would I? I'm a Indian, not a White woman. Here,
read for me."

They all looked over Daylily's shoulder while she read, as
if they knew what the words said. "It say, 'To Pri-vate Clar-
ence Ol-m-stead, Con-fed-derate pr-isoner of war, Eden, North
Caro-lina Cole Pitts.' What's 'Cole Pitts,' Miz Betty?"

"Coal's for burnin," Betty answered. "Got to dig down
underground to get it out. What the letter say?"

"It say, 'My dear Clar-ence. I'm pray the letter reach you

and that you are in soun health in that reb prison. We hear about the sick-nesses that has taken more than three [[zero-zerozero, I don know what that sum is, y'all]] of our boys who would be happier dyin for the cose, but die instead for small-pox.'"

Suddenly Betty knew what it was she was looking at. "Get back in the house!" she said. "Bring me some old rags and drop them by the woodpile. Don't touch nothin in the house till I git there! Now git!"

She had to call on her relations. The ground was telling her things. Broken leaves, dragged dust. Look like he had gone outside for some reason. This Union man, he wasn't one of those who had caught her two days ago. She had never seen his face before. This man looked too sick to do anything but die.

One bad thing followed another, and now another bad thing had to be done. She had to get these children out of here before that scum came back looking for her. There was always that chance, and with smallpox . . . There wasn't any way she could fix it so they could stay.

She made a little pillow with the rags and put it under Olmsted's head. Went to the pump and washed and scrubbed her hands as clean as she could with lemongrass and cold water and then lye soap she kept at the pump. She should have known they could only stay with her for so long, but her heart hurt, knowing what she had to do, hurt for them and for herself.

"Miz Betty!" Daylily called from the house. "We hungry!"

Inside the cabin, she looked at everything real hard. The three children were sitting on the floor waiting for her just like she had told them. "OK, here's what we gotta do," she said. "First we gotta eat, and then we gotta talk, and then we gotta rest."

"But Miz Betty," Caswell said, getting ready to ask the question they were all thinking. "What about the poor sick man? You gonna leave him in the yard like that?"

She took Caswell and set him on her lap. "Come'ere, Gray Wolf. You all need to know. This man's more'n likely got the smallpox, but I ain't sure yet."

"See," Luke said to Daylily, "I tole you!"

"Shh, Luke. Just listen. That's terrible bad sickness for him and bad news for us, whatever it is. Cause you guys gotta grow up, and if he gives you the sickness, you might not get to. You might get sick and die. So after we eat, I gonna find somewhere in the woods for you to sleep, and next day you gotta rest, and then you gotta go."

They all looked like she had slapped them. She hated this. She purely hated it, what she had to do, and all the heart went out of her.

"Go where?" said Caswell.

"Go north like you was before I found you and you found me."

"We gotta leave you?" Daylily looked like that was the last thing on earth she thought Betty would ever say. "No, I don't wanna. Betty, we can't leave without you, we can't!" Daylily put her arms around Betty and held on tight.

Luke said softly, "She can't help it. We catch that man's sickness we all gon die."

Tears were brightening Daylily's brown eyes. "But Betty, Miz Betty, what you gon do?" she said.

"Don't you worry bout Miz Betty Strong Foot, Little Bear.

Got plenty strong medicine," she said, beating her chest and making fun of how White men sometimes talked to her, pretending to be brave. But she wasn't, not brave at all. This was harder than being captured.

"But you'll die," Caswell wailed.

"Betty not gon die!" she said. "Promise. Now stop that and let's get somethin to eat. Some good meat and bread. And then I gotta talk to Luke. I got somethin for him to do." Everyone looked anxious and scared. "Listen, everything gon work out. You gonna get up north, you gonna grow up and be important people, and you gonna come back here and see Betty someday. I gonna show you a way to get to Harper's Ferry, and you kin get help there, have a place to stay, and find some grown folks to take care of you. I gonna show you which way to go, so don't be scared. And some day y'all gonna be all grown up doin all kinda important things in the world.

"Now listen to Betty. All of you got strong medicine. Caswell is a wolf. A wolf is a teacher; he finds a way, and he can always get back home to the family. Wolf must lead by sharing what he learns. And he teaches other people what he learned. Wolves be loyal and wise.

"And Daylily is a bear. A bear knows things by listenin. Bear goes to the dream lodge and tells us the truth. Bear is a fierce mother for the young."

Daylily's chin was trembling, but she was trying hard to be brave.

"And Luke," said Betty, "Luke got powerful eagle medicine. Luke got big courage. He can come through fiery trials. He can fly high and see it all. He knows the whole story, and he talks to the Great Spirit and tells other folks. So you see, you got everything you need. What did I say? If you believe, you ain't never alone. You got a whole passel of angels and spirit animals with you. And you gotta be caring for each other."

Daylily blew her nose on a handkerchief and straightened her shoulders. She put her arm around Caswell. "We can do it for you, Miz Betty," she said.

That's all Betty could say to them, and she hoped and prayed they had strength enough to make it without her. "You all gotta promise Betty you gonna be strong, OK?" Caswell nodded, yes. Luke made a fist and said, "OK, OK, Betty, we gon be fine."

Betty pointed at each one of them. "Cause you a bear, an eagle and a wolf, and that's a fact!" she said. "I saw it in my sleep, and what I see in my sleep I believe!"

They ate quickly; in spite of their trouble, they were all hungry, like children almost always are. Every few minutes, Betty would look outside and go around back to where the sick man was. Yaller Feet came stepping back from wherever he had gone. He must have run when the sick man came around. "Checkin up," she told them. "Got to be on the lookout."

They had to go rest in the woods on the back side of the house away from the soldier, so she could watch for them. About thirty yards from the house Betty knew there was a small cave. She took the children there and gave them a quilt to lie on, and put another quilt over them to keep the chill away. When she walked away, she felt a big lump in her throat. These my children, she thought. They deserve something more than this.

While they were resting, she put together some food for the road, and water in the canteens. She gave Luke fresh gunpowder in his powder bag, and cleaned his rifle. She made a sling to make it easier for him to carry his rifle, and then she went outside and woke Luke up.

He had dozed off, and she was glad he had been able to get some sleep. They were all tired from their rescue efforts.

"Luke, you gotta wake up," Betty said, hating to wake him.

He rubbed his eyes. "Huh?" he mumbled. "Yeah?"

"I'm sorry, little Blue Eagle, you gotta do one more piece of business for me before y'all go. You gotta take a message. It's two hours walkin time, where you gotta go. I need you to carry these words in your head, OK? The words are 'Red is dead. Sunrise on the left.' OK?"

"Red is dead. Sunrise on the left," Luke said to himself slowly. Then all of a sudden he was fully awake. He knew she was giving him a spy message! He was both thrilled and scared.

"Now," she said. "Listen good, Luke. You go back to the house where they caught me, only don't go all the way. Stop at the cornfield before the house. It'll be an old cornfield gone to seed. You know the difference between right and left?"

Luke nodded.

"Put out your right hand." Luke did as he was told.

"Now put out your left hand. That's it. The old cornfield on the left hand. Now come outside a minute."

Betty pointed to a tree at the edge of the yard. "You see that tree? This old house about from here to that tree. Is gonna be a man there at sundown tonight in the cornfield. Old Black man, white hair, and beard, tall. He gonna whistle 'John Brown's Body.' You know that song?"

Luke shook his head. "I'm not sure, Betty."

"I'll hum it for you," she said.

As she sang the song for him, he seemed to remember it and began to hum along. He said Unc Steph used to hum it under his breath, but he had never heard anybody but Betty sing the words.

"Sing it for me," Betty said. And she hummed it again, so he could follow. When she thought he had it, she said, "When you hear the song, you say the words. Now what are they? Tell me again."

Luke repeated the "red is dead" message.

"Don't say these words to *nobody* else, you hear? *Nobody!* If you do, they tie you up and take you to jail, or worse. If you see somebody else sides the old man, you hide, and hightail it back here soon as you can. I can't go cause they know me now. They caught me. Folks be on the lookout for me. We just gotta get this message there. It'll save a lot of lives on both sides, I hope. You gotta leave now. You just got time."

"Betty, I's just wonderin, is it Union or reb this message is for?"

"For both. We's trying to stop a battle. One way or nother, it don't matter to me."

But Luke was stubborn, and he knew right from wrong even at his age.

But Betty knew he wasn't old enough to know that right and wrong could sometimes get so they looked like they were all mixed up, even if they weren't. He wasn't old enough to know folks could lose their faith in most everything and just decide to live the best way they could and the devil take the rest. He was not old enough to know bitterness.

"But Miz Betty, it got to matter. Don't you see? It got to! I don't wanna be helpin no rebs. They hate my kind. They

treat us like dogs! Don't you see? It ain't right! It ain't
right!"

Daylily and Caswell were stirring from their naps. They
had heard most of the conversation between Betty and Luke,
and sat up on the quilt, a little confused but knowing Luke
was going somewhere without them. Betty could see the fear
on Daylily's face.

"Where he goin, Miz Betty? You can't send him away. He
got to go to Harper's Ferry with us. We can't make it without
him! And we got to stay out here in this cave by ourselves!"

Caswell nodded, knowing that at least what Daylily said
was true. They couldn't make it without Luke.

Betty patted Daylily's shoulder to soothe her. "Shh, you
gon be fine," she said quietly. She was just praying he'd make
it back. So many lives depended on this one little boy doing a
job she should have done if she just hadn't been captured!

"Shh," she said, trying to put their fears to rest. "He comin
back, tonight! And I gonna be looking in on you all night.
Don't you worry; you and Caswell be fine. Luke just goin for
a little while."

Luke was crying now, but he wiped his face with an angry
swipe of his sleeve.

"Hush now, Luke, husha bye," Betty said, taking his hand.
"I know you got eagle medicine in you, aiming for the sky,
ain't that so? It's all right. This for Union. Betty sees the sky
you be flyin in, Little Blue Eagle."

Luke nodded that he understood. At least Betty seemed to
know why he couldn't be a spy for the rebs.

"You go now. Time movin too fast already. The Great Spirit
hold you up and Betty will sing you there and back."

"Bye, Luke," Daylily said, talking barely above a whisper. "You got your mama's mojo?"

"Yeah, course I do."

"Bye, Luke," echoed Caswell. "You got your rifle?"

"You my brother now, Caswell, don't you forget," Luke answered.

"Sho nuff, Luke."

"Yeah, that's a fact," answered Luke. He needed to hurry up and go before he got to crying again. He wanted to be proud and tall, and act like a man, even though he felt more like a child leaving his mama.

"Be there by sundown," Betty called out to him as he vanished into the woods. "Remember, the eagle is always nearby and the Great Spirit be by your side."

CHAPTER 25

CLARENCE OLMSTEAD

During that evening while Luke was gone, Betty didn't even try to sleep. She kept walking to the cave and back to check on Daylily and Caswell. Worry kept knocking at the door of her mind. Where was Luke, how was he doing, was he on his way back by now? Full night came, and no Luke. She really did have to be brave now, for the sake of the younger children. Daylily was restless. Once she woke up calling for Betty while Betty was standing over her to make sure she was covered with the quilt. "I'm here, Little Bear," she said. "Don't you fret yourself. Betty ain't gonna let nothing happen to you all. Luke be back soon. You rest now." Daylily lay back again and Betty tucked the quilt tighter around her.

She went back to the cabin and tried to work on a special blanket that she was weaving, with images of the wolf, the bear and the eagle, but she couldn't concentrate. The last thing she wanted to do was leave them alone with a sick and maybe dying man to go looking for Luke. No telling if other soldiers or that trash was looking for her, and to add to everything else, Clarence Olmstead seemed to be even worse. He was sweating so. His whole face was wet. He was talking out of his head. She took pity on him and dragged him into the house as far away from their beds as possible.

It was hard work, but it was a good thing he was so skinny and Betty was strong, because he was almost dead weight. Betty listened to his ravings to see if she could hear anything about the troops, and where he'd come from.

Suddenly he opened his eyes like he was staring at a vision; he muttered something about his boy. "My son," he kept saying, "my only son, dead by a rebel bullet, twelve years old, and dead . . ." and then he sank back into his fever.

Betty looked around for a rag she could throw away later. She went to wet it under the pump out back, and came back to wipe the sweat off his face. He must have sensed her standing over him, and he started and opened his eyes, yelling out "David, David!"

"Just you rest now," she said aloud.

But Clarence Olmstead fell back in a stupor again.

Poor man, Betty thought. Lost his son. The longer she sat there, the more she thought of Luke and what danger he might be in. "I must be ailing in my mind," she said to herself, "to send him into such danger."

And he said he wouldn't mind if it meant something, if it meant something to the others he had loved. He had more sense than she had, more than she ever had. He really was an eagle, flying up there close to God. She had named him without even knowing how right she was. Betty sat up straight in her rocking chair. She wiped the man's forehead, and thought of this poor man and his son and Luke.

If she sent Luke, whom she loved like he was her own child, to be murdered by some no-count dirty dogs, it had to be for something, something that really mattered like breaking slavery chains, setting free all the suffering people who were tortured and murdered, treated like animals or worse. She didn't know about that life firsthand because God had blessed her with a life of freedom, but she knew from her papa how terrible it would be to have somebody own you. Why didn't I see, she thought, why didn't I see until now?

"Oh, Lord, oh, God, oh, Great Spirit," she prayed, "send my chile home to me." She sat by Olmstead all night and rocked and chanted in her mama's words for Luke's safe homecoming. And she knew, she knew now for sure. There would be no more spying for the rebs, not from her, not ever again.

Rocking and rocking and wiping her tears, she said, finally, "It's all right, Luke, it's all right. And Lord, just get him back here so I can tell him I know. I know what he was cryin about. He wanted me to know that we gotta be strong and stand up for right. Oh, Great Spirit, if you really listening to Betty Strong Foot, send him back to us so's I can tell him Betty knows, we got to stand, we got to stand till all our people be free."

CHAPTER 26

RED IS DEAD.
SUNRISE ON THE LEFT.

Help me, Jesus," he said over and over as he trudged down the road. Once he got out of sight of Betty and his friends, it was easier. He could concentrate on the river. "Follow the river, that's all I have to do," he said to himself. "It'll be easy and I'll be there in two shakes." He looked up at the sun, and it was on its way toward night, but he would make it. He just couldn't stop and rest. If Caswell could find his way all alone, he could sure do it.

"Red is dead. Sunrise on the left," he kept saying to himself. He practiced it as many different ways as he could imagine it. How would it sound if President Lincoln said it to the soldiers? How would it sound if Robert E. Lee said it to his troops? Would he be sad cause it'd mean they had lost? And wouldn't Unc Steph be proud of him for being a spy for the Union? He couldn't have done this much for freedom if he had gone to fight. That thought made him shiver. Like as not he would have ended up like some of them dead soldiers he'd seen.

River turns kinda right, here soon, he thought, and I'll be

maybe halfway. Something moved along the riverbank, and a brown snake showed its head. Luke edged around it slowly and kept moving, but he picked up a big stick just in case, and patted his rifle. The snake moved on. Lots more smells of autumn now than when he ran away from Massa Higsaw. That seemed like a whole year ago, he thought.

Locusts whined their early evening song. Getting late, Luke thought. He pulled out some of Betty's corn bread and chewed it while he walked. Then he began to notice something different. He couldn't quite pin it down at first. Something . . . a smell . . . It was a smell.

Then he heard something that he hadn't heard when they came home early this afternoon. It was sounds of people. He would have sworn it was people, but he couldn't see anybody anywhere. It was just a low hum, buzzing around, wagon wheels, men's voices, horses neighing. Something has happened since first light this mornin, he thought. He believed it before he could see it. The sounds got clearer and clearer, and he smelled the mixture of smoke, horse manure and unwashed men very distinctly.

"Oh, Lordy," whispered Luke. He wrapped his fingers around his mojo, saying whatever prayers came to his mind. He felt his rifle for comfort. He thought they were really close. A whole passel of soldiers. Would they be Union or reb? He started to sweat with fear. It ran down his forehead. He wiped it with his arm and kept moving. His feet were really hurting, and he wanted to rest, but the sun was very low now. He wondered if Betty knew about the soldiers moving in. Maybe she did, maybe not. And would the old bearded man still meet him in the cornfield?

• • •

I can't fail, he thought, I can't let folks down. He had been so distracted by the soldiers that it took him by surprise. There it was, the farmhouse up ahead and the cornfield on the left. "Red is dead, red is dead, sunrise, sunrise . . . sunrise, sunrise . . . on the left," he repeated to himself. His mind was blank except for that.

He didn't see a soul. What if nobody came? Or somebody else came instead? Here he was standing by a cornfield with nothing but a big stick and a rifle. They could shoot him down without so much as a howdy-do.

Suddenly Luke heard a scream, but it came from above him. He looked up into the darkening sky, afraid for his life. A black shadow circled high over his head. What he saw he would never forget. It was a huge bird, and he realized it was an eagle. Betty said I was an eagle, he thought. She said I ain't afraid of nothing. She said I am like the eagle, strong, and close to Spirit, and I ain't afraid of nothing. The eagle circled a minute or two, and then it flew off into the distance. He knew then that the eagle had come to help him get through this, to tell him he would be all right.

He calmed down some, and he heard the voices of soldiers, some drilling and some yelling. They must be right around here real close, he thought. The sun was leaning on the horizon now. Then he heard rustling, and something rose out of the corn like a haint rising from the dead. His legs would not move. He was frozen to the spot. And his breath was so caught in his nose and mouth that it nearly choked him. The thing was tall, and thin, and it looked all black like him, like a spirit from the other side, until he saw the white beard.

He realized it was a Black man, and he let his breath out so fast it made him dizzy. His head was swimming. Then he heard the whistle—the tune to "John Brown's Body." Soft and low like nobody was supposed to hear it. The man came closer to him, but he didn't seem to really look at him. "Red is dead," Luke breathed out. He took a breath between each word. "Sunrise on the left." That was all. Oh, Lordy, he thought, did I get it right?

The man turned and then he was gone, like he had never been there. Just melted into the dark, didn't walk, just melted and was gone. So it was done. Luke stood there in the dark, amazed to be alive and still breathing. In his mind he kept seeing the eagle's dark shadow flying over his head like an angel. The eagle is nearby, he thought, always nearby.

Suddenly he was so hungry he could barely stand it. But it was too spooky out there to eat the rest of his bread, and he needed to pee badly before he started out for Betty's cabin. Right here next to the corn would be fine since nobody was around.

I did it, he thought. I did it! He felt like letting out a big holler, just cause he was still alive! But he was fastening his trousers one minute, and the next minute he was dangling from someone's arm and yelling bloody murder.

CHAPTER 27

JOHN BROWN'S BODY

Wﾍhat is it, Mr. Simpson? Is it a nigger?" said a voice that might as well have come from the devil himself.

"Boy, what are you doing way out here by yourself?" said the man who was holding him.

Luke just struggled to get himself free.

"Well, Corporal, we'll just have to see him in the light of the fire cause we can't see his face in this here moonlight, now can we? Be still, boy, and stop that thrashin."

"This is a dark young'un, sure enough, Mr. Simpson. What you say we roast him for dinner?"

"Naw, he'd be too tough," the other one laughed. "And I'll be damned if he isn't armed too, a nigger boy with a rifle!" They took his gun and his water.

By that time Luke was fighting with all his might. "That's mine," he screamed. "Give that back!"

One of them held his arm so he couldn't hit them, but Luke still kicked as wildly as he could.

"Well, now, we just gonna have to put him outta his misery if he continues to kick, won't we, Corporal? Boy, you know you stole this here gun. You want me to knock you silly?"

Luke stopped kicking. There was no telling what these men would do to him. At least they were Union, he figured because of their blue caps. Their trousers were filthy and their shirts were some muddy color. Maybe they would really kill him if he didn't obey them. If he had just left there right away! If he had just not stopped to pee! He could hear his own breathing in the space between their words.

"You coming with us," one of them said. "We gotta take you in. Quick march! One-two-three-four, one-two-three-four." They held him by the arms and made him march with them.

They were headed in the direction of the soldiers. Then Luke saw them, what looked like thousands of white tents in the moonlight, just around the bend from the river, and thousands of little cooking fires, and it would have been a beautiful sight if he hadn't been scared senseless by the two men who had captured him.

Then he remembered Betty had told him they'd tie him up and put him in jail, or worse. "Oh, Jesus," he prayed silently, "please don't let them kill me. Please don't let them hang me."

"Well, Mr. Simpson," said one of the men as they got near the camp, "I'm thinking we better let the boys know about our prize. Just what was you doin out here in that field in the night anyway, young'un?"

Luke shook his head. He wasn't telling them. Never.

"Don't wanna talk," the corporal said. "OK, we'll see about that." They dragged him to a tent and tied his arms and legs together so he couldn't walk or move around much.

"Now you'll stay put. Come tomorrow's battle you can carry water for us. We'll be needin plenty to fight them Johnny Rebs, nasty as they be. And maybe we'll let them eat you too, if you don't tell us what you was doing in that cornfield."

Praise the Lord, they hated rebs, but they still weren't let-ting him go. And then he remembered that Betty had said, "Don't tell nobody else."

They were talking right outside the tent flap. Their captain was with them. Now Luke see could only their shadows through the tent, but he could hear them clearly.

"Somebody here been carrying tales, you understand me, Captain?" said one of the men who'd captured him. "They always seem to know where we gonna be ahead of time. I hear the rebs been using women and children, anybody they can get lately. Could be this boy's one of them. You know darkies. Give em a piece of biscuit, and a warm place to sleep, and they'll do anything for you."

"Right strange, ain't it," said the captain through his teeth. Luke saw the glow of his cigarette through the tent flap. "He was out there alone at night, nobody with him, no house in sight except that abandoned barn and farmhouse. What's he say he was doing?"

"Don't open his mouth, Captain. Want me to beat it out of him?"

"Not yet. Let me think on it awhile. See what the other boys dug up while they was on watch. It might be we can use him if we can scare him good enough. Give em something, they'll change sides just like that," he said, snapping his fin-gers. "Ain't got sense enough to know it's in their best interest to work with us."

Somewhere a shot rang out. In the tent, Luke jumped. But nothing happened. After a while, he went to sleep, exhausted with worry and fear.

He was dreaming of home—of Aunt Eugenia, and some-how Betty and Daylily and Caswell were in the dream too.

Then someone was pushing and shaking him. "Hey, wake up, boy, wake up, you! Captain wants to see your black behind."

A man with a thin nose and a stubbly beard took the ropes off his arms and legs, which were really sore now. "Come with me, you."

Luke blinked, getting used to the glare of the rising sun. He had a terrible headache. His mouth was sour and dry. All he wanted to do was go back to Betty's, but something was happening.

It was barely dawn. Soldiers were sitting, standing, walking around, but not lounging. They were alert, as if waiting for something. The man dragging Luke along by the wrist stepped in front of another and said, "Captain, here's the Negro you wanted to see."

"Boy," said the captain, "I could use me a good runner during the battle." Luke looked up at the tall, thin White man with a brown mustache. He held up something that gleamed in the light. "See this coin? It's yours if you tell me just what you were doing out there in the dark. And if you don't tell me, I just might feed you to them rebs over there across the way. So what do you say? What's it to be? Me or them?"

On the whole, Luke thought, lying wasn't worth the trouble it caused later. Plus, Aunt Eugenia said it was a sin. But this was a special case. Saying a little prayer that God wouldn't mind, he looked innocently at the captain and said, "Sir, I was just trying to get to the Union side to join up." And that wasn't exactly a lie. "I always wanted to fight for the Union, suh, and I was following my Unc Steph, cause he done left home to join up. So I got lost, Captain, suh."

"So I see. And you weren't by any chance trying to give special information to our enemies? And you weren't by any chance sent here so you could tell the rebs where we were? Boy, how long you been following my boys to get the food they left behind? You been stealing?"

He fired the questions so fast that Luke was afraid to answer any of them. "No, suh," he said, because he thought that was the safest thing to do. Just say no to all questions.

Suddenly it looked like the army was on the move. "Oh, hell, what am I doing questioning a Black boy the size of a turnip?" said the captain.

A few guns rang out. Someone yelled, and they were in it. A battle was about to start. Luke heard the rattle-tapping of the drummers, and everyone and everything around him started to change position. Wagons of cannonballs were being pulled by horses, men were running everywhere, and some were yelling orders. Through the dust Luke saw huge cannons being drawn up by mules and then men would push them into position for firing.

"Here, boy," the captain said as he flipped the coin to Luke. "It's yours. Now, see that gentleman on the brown and white horse?" He pointed through the trees. "Run over there, and tell him you're a new runner for the lines. He can use you to do anything he needs doing. Try to stay with him while the battle's going on." It was getting so noisy that Luke could hardly hear the captain. "Tell him your name, boy," the captain called out in all the confused mass of men and noise. "Tell him your name!"

Amazed at himself, Luke was obedient. He forgot for a moment how scared he was, and how he wanted to be with the others at Betty's cabin. He was caught up in the flags and yells, and the colors and smoke coming together. If Unc Steph could just see him now! They wouldn't think he was too young. They'd never think it again!

He was running, trying to catch up with the man who was too busy even to know he was there, and called out. "I'm a runner for the lines! Luke, suh, it's Luke!" He was running alongside the horse as best he could, but the soldier never heard him. And just as he looked back to ask the captain with the mustache what to do, everything broke loose.

Men and horses were running pell-mell in all directions, and suddenly some men ran into him, knocking Luke down. A soldier howled, and bits of bone covered in blood were on Luke's arms and something grainy was in his hands. He scrambled up and ran again into the dust and mud.

He was not able to see where he was headed because of the smoke and always the noise, the noise that was everywhere bigger than anything he knew, bigger than the whole sky. The noise was unbearable, and then he fell headlong into rough brown grass. Just then he saw the captain.

A thundering sound hit Luke, the captain's face exploded, and he fell heavily into the dust. Luke's mouth was opened with the explosion, so that he swallowed smoke and something vile went under his tongue. He saw bright orange cannon fire exploding through the smoke. Someone let out a piercing scream, and he wondered who was working his arms and legs. He only knew he had to get away from the noise, and oh, God, the captain's face was there and then it was gone. He ran forward in the direction those who were around him seemed to be going.

These were his arms, he thought. These were his legs, and it was not his face that had been blown to bits, not his face.

Now the noise was not so terrible. He touched his face. He shut his eyes, praying, praying, afraid to see, afraid he had landed in a place worse than before, afraid the noise would start again.

The battle raged. The noise hit again. Men swayed forward in confusion. Luke found himself on the ground, and someone ran over his legs. He struggled up, and his legs seemed to move on their own. He stumbled over a man who was clutching his stomach, and the man's blood sprayed into Luke's face. He ran ahead again. He didn't know why he was running, he only knew he had to keep going. He was tired, so tired. He was out of breath, and he only wanted to lie down and rest, and who was this running, he wondered, and he felt something wet on his nose and his face. Jesus, not his nose, or was it the captain's nose he saw, past smoke and dead and dying horses, smoke and mud, and then he saw a black face and a white beard. He heard the song above all the noise, "John Brown's body lies a-molderin in the grave." He heard the words and saw the dark man beckoning him to come, and he did. It was as if something lifted him up, and he heard himself now, praying, with his eyes closed tight, "Jesus, keep me near the cross, please keep me," and he wondered, Who is that screaming, oh, God, make it go away.

Then the noise was almost gone, and Luke wondered how he'd gotten there on this grass by himself. He opened his eyes and saw his own brown arms and hands, and he felt his legs, and his face. It was covered with mud and blood that came off on his hands. And where was the old man who had shown him the way? Where was the old man who had sung "John Brown's Body"? He had been there, and then he was not there. Must have been one of those angels that Betty talks about, he thought.

Luke could still see the men fighting. He had run as far as he could before he fell. He looked at the men in the distance. He felt like he was in a dream. The horses still screamed and fell to their deaths, trapping men underneath them; the cannon kept booming, but the noises were muffled. They were far away now, but did he dare to move?

Luke felt something in his pocket, and there was the coin, the gold coin from the captain. It was really there, and it had all really happened, all of it. His rifle was gone, and his canteen. He could still hear guns and screaming men, and then he burst out, "Oh, Lordy! Daylily and Caswell and Betty Strong Foot!" They'd be thinking he was dead!

He stood there and looked at the valley in front of him, at the sea of death. He watched men crumple like dolls. One soldier grabbed the Union flag from his dead friend and ran forward into the smoke, and he watched men thrust their bayonets into each other.

Something kept him standing there looking at the men in their struggle to live and die. He fingered the gold piece and thought, That man is dead now. A man who had walked and talked and given him the coin, that man's face was in pieces on the ground, and he was dead now. "Your name," the captain had called out. "Tell him your name!" And then his face was blown away, and he was dead.

Luke watched the battle for a long time. He felt sad for the captain and for all the men who were still dying out there, and he felt like he had failed and had left them to die. He cried silently and let the tears roll down his face. He felt old.

CHAPTER 28

SUMMER FAREWELL

Luke could see the river flowing along peacefully as if the hours he had just lived through were not real, as if there had been no Black man in the cornfield, no soldiers and no battle. During the walk back to Betty's cabin he felt different. He didn't believe he would be scared of anything as long as he lived.

He reached Betty's cabin sometime after what his stomach told him was past time to eat, and he was starving. He hadn't eaten since last night in the cornfield. Suddenly, he just couldn't go another step, and he was terribly thirsty and shaking. "Hey there, hey y'all!" he cried out. But he didn't see anybody. "Hey, Miz Betty! Hey, Caswell, Daylily, I'm home!"

Betty's door opened slowly. She held up her hand as if to stop his coming. "Don't come near, Luke," she yelled. "Don't come in here no farther. Smallpox is here. I'm sure now. This man's got it!"

"Where's everybody?" he yelled.

"They in the woods," she called back. "In the cave where

you left them. You call out and they'll come." She pointed him in the right direction.

"Betty?" he yelled. "Betty, I did my job, Betty!"

She smiled. It was the first time he remembered Betty smiling a real smile. "That's one for the Union, Luke!" she said from across the yard.

The cave was easy to find, and he called out to his friends like the returning soldier he was. Daylily and Caswell were on him like puppies welcoming their owner, full of questions and excitement.

All Luke wanted to do was eat and sleep. Betty made squirrel stew and brought it to them, and Luke stuffed himself, all the while telling them what had happened. And then he slept like a dead person. Betty wouldn't get too close or let them touch her, and though she let them alone tonight because of Luke's homecoming, she knew they'd have to leave very soon, maybe tomorrow. Smallpox was just too dangerous. Besides, she had put them all in danger by stabbing that ruffian and taking the horse and wagon, and tomorrow would make the third day since she had been captured.

She went into the cabin, her mind so occupied with the children that she forgot she needed to stop at the pump for some water. She needed to fill her bucket. She lifted her lantern and took it with her. Out back, the pump creaked and water trickled out. She was squatting at the pump for better traction. But the sound of the water was not the only sound she heard.

She heard Cetto, the mother rattler. Betty had not forgotten seeing the snake just before the children came to her. She froze. In the light thrown by the lantern, she could make out the huge brown snake in the shadows as it slid out of the woodpile. She didn't dare turn her head, but she could see out of the corner of her eye; the snake was watching her.

The rattle sounded its dreadful warning. Mother Cetto rose up and looked at Betty. And then quietly changing her mind, she lowered her head and slithered away silently.

A few seconds passed. Betty stood up very slowly, very quietly. She was sure now. It was time for them to go. As hard as it was to do, she was doing the right thing.

On her way back to the house, she looked up at the sky. Clouds moved and covered the new moon, and somewhere something rumbled. Guns, she thought, or thunder, and she was sure hoping it wasn't thunder, because she hated to send those children out in rain. Maybe two days longer, maybe then was soon enough. "Does it ever come easy?" she asked the gathering clouds. "Does it ever come easy to let go of somebody you love?"

The wind blew a leaf into her face. The November chill had really settled in now, and as she went inside to tend to her sick guest, the tears were running down her face. Just as well, she thought. Just as well I cry now instead of having them see me cry when they go. No more warm weather. Now Indian summer was gone for sure.

CHAPTER 29

FOLLOW THE RIVER

It had been half an hour since they'd left Betty Strong Foot, and nobody could say anything. All Luke heard was Daylily sniffling, and Caswell sobbing, and he was wiping his own tears away so he could see where they were going. The rain had left the woods dripping, but at least the sun was out good and strong.

"I don't care, it's cold out here," Caswell said all of a sudden. "I'm going back." He had on a pair of moccasins Betty had made when she made the shirts and pants and jackets for all of them. Even colder weather would be here soon, she'd said, and they needed things for the night.

Daylily carried a small quilt rolled up and strapped to her back. Betty had said it should take them three or four days to get to Harper's Ferry, where they could find some people who could help them. She said she couldn't spy any more, and that would mean they wouldn't have enough food.

Luke thought there would be some grown folks who'd be sure to send them back to where the rebs could get at them and split them up. And maybe they'd never see each other again. He didn't say it out loud because he didn't want to scare the others, but he knew Daylily was thinking of that too, and just wasn't saying it.

"Naw," Luke said to Caswell, "you can't go back there. Betty says we'll get the smallpox and die."

"How come she won't die?" Caswell looked at Luke.

With that long hair, he did look like a little Indian, Luke thought, he was so browned from the sun.

"Cause she ain't!" Luke answered. "Cause she say so. She got ways. Anyway, we got to keep movin forward. It's danger in these parts. I ought know. I sho nuff been in it."

Daylily was way ahead of them now. She called back over her shoulder. "She got to move on, long as the war lasts, so she won't git kilt! And hang from a tree! So come on! Both of y'all."

The shadows were long now, and they stopped walking as if they had reached a silent agreement.

"Guess we should eat some of this Betty give us," said Day-lily. "She said it was enough for four days." Daylily divided up Caswell's bread and dried fish into four parts and gave him back one part.

They sat down and ate in silence, everyone sad and afraid to say how much they hurt. The unthinkable had happened. They were looking for a home again, alone, and it was almost worse than before because they had lost Betty. They gathered wood for a fire, but their hearts were not in it. They were slow and listless.

"When I get to where we's goin, I ain't never gon leave home again, whatever home is," Daylily said between her bites. "What's that place, Harper's Terry?"

"Harper's Ferry," Luke answered.

"Well, what's that anyway?" said Caswell. "I bet it won't be half as good as Betty's place."

"It's a town," Luke said. "That's all I know about it."

Daylily looked up from her meal, which was all but gone. "Is it any colored folks there?"

"I spect it's colored folks everywhere," Luke said. "Don't you?"

"Not in Heaven," said Caswell.

Luke turned, suddenly and fiercely, and faced Caswell. "I done already tole you. My mama is there," he said quietly, "and don't you never say that again." He lay facedown on his jacket.

"Luke, it's just cause . . . cause, well, how come I never seen a picture of a Black angel? They're always White in our Sunday school Bible. Mamadear had White angels on her wall and . . . I'm really sorry, Luke . . . I just . . ."

"Just shut up, OK? Just shut up."

"Anyway, we ain't goin to no Heaven," said Daylily quickly, looking sideways at Luke. "We goin to that town, Harper's Ferry, and it's plenty colored folks there, I bet."

Caswell looked at Luke, but Luke had turned his head away. Daylily refilled the canteen with river water and offered some to Luke. After a few minutes, he seemed to feel better, and they settled into their all-too-familiar routine of making a campfire.

"What you gon do in Harper's Ferry, Luke?" said Daylily. "Do you reckon we's gonna get put in jail or somethin bad for runnin away?"

"Don't know." He shrugged his thin shoulders. "Depends on the war, I reckon. On rebs and Union. Massa Higsaw was about dead when I left, sick and drunk all the time; you ain't got no people no more at your place, and Caswell, his mama dead. They got to find his daddy, if he ain't kilt in the war, you know. I might join up with the Union if I can find some soldiers when us gets to Harper's Ferry."

"You mean fight? Like a soldier? You get killed, Luke, sure as huntin dogs holler. You get killed, and then I ain't got a friend in the world. And Caswell gon be with some White folks, that's for sure. I done heard you say it before, but that was before we was friends, you know." She poked in the dirt with a twig.

Luke was silent, and kept gathering twigs. He didn't know what to say about Daylily's gloomy picture of the future, but maybe he could just work around the camps. A lot had happened to him, and he was still alive. Maybe she was right and he would only be killed in the war.

He didn't care what Caswell said, his mam was in Heaven and she was an angel. He bet there were other Black angels there too. And if he got killed, he'd see his mam again in her right mind.

"My daddy ain't dead," Caswell insisted. "He'll come and get me."

Nobody answered him.

"What you gon do when we get to Harper's Ferry, Daylily?" Luke asked. He was curious about what a girl would say.

"Work, I reckon. Like I always been doin." She was very quiet after that; for a long time they only listened to the fire and cracked twigs with their fingers.

Finally, Luke said what he had been thinking. "You reckon us could find a way to be together?"

"Maybe," she said, "if you don't get shot up in the war. Maybe us could work on a Harper's Ferry plantation."

"Maybe they don't have plantations there. Aunt Eugenia, she say in a town, it be lots of houses and buildings, more'n you ever saw. Lots of people in these buildings, and maybe us work in one of those White folks' houses. When the Yankees win, we gonna be free and get paid to work."

"Maybe," whispered Daylily.

"My papa find me, I bet," said Caswell. "I just bet he will."

Luke knew it was time to go to sleep if they were going to make good time in the morning, but he wasn't sleepy for some reason. Daylily was also wide awake. They stretched out on their quilt, using their army coats for some protection against the dampness. It was warm close to the fire, and they both looked straight up through the darkness. They were close enough to the river to hear the water lapping against the bank, and they could smell the damp moss and mold of decaying leaves. The sky was very clear of clouds.

"I wonder what gon happen to us for real," Daylily whispered.

"Me too," Luke echoed. "Two more days good walkin and we be there. Sure is a big Heaven up there. Look at all them stars."

"It's big, that's a fact. Big as this here woods, I reckon." Daylily looked over at Caswell, who had fallen fast asleep. "Then Caswell's mama be up there too. Could be right next to your mama lookin down on us. They be up there with my granny. Three of them up there together, three of us down here together."

They were quiet for a minute or two, thinking about what she had said. "Luke, if you go to fight in the war, how you gonna find us? We best friends. We like brother and sister."

"I thought you said I be dead."

"Well, maybe you ain't kilt. And if you ain't kilt, how you gon find us? And Caswell, God only know where the White folks'll take him." Daylily's voice got very small then. "And Luke, if they sells us away, we won't never be able to see each other again. You, me, Caswell, we's like family. How'm I gonna find you all in this big world?"

"We got to have a pact. That's it. Like folks do when they runnin away to freedom. We got to have a plan. We got to remember to meet up when we get grown. To meet up like I was tryin to meet up with Unc Steph and Gustavus and Junior Boy to go to the war. I had a plan, only they wasn't there at the tree, or else I was late. I don know. But that's what we gotta do. Now this here year is eighteen hundred and sixty-four. So in ten more summers we meet up."

"Suppose we ain't free? Suppose the rebs win the war? Then we be runnin away from the massa."

"You be grown up," Luke said. "It'll be easier. And anyway, the Union gonna win this war. I just know they is. And you be free. You can go anywhere you want then."

Daylily turned over on her stomach and took her favorite position, her head on her fists. "Where us gon meet though? Us could meet at Betty's house. When us get to Harper's Ferry, we see where the river goes, and just turn around and go back to Betty's. Can you count on your fingers, Luke? I can count. Granny learned me that too. Count it on your fingers—one, two, three, four, five, six, seven, eight, nine, ten. That's a lot of summers, ain't it, Luke? Luke?"

He had fallen into a dream while she was counting to ten. In his sleep he could hear her counting, only he was counting stars, and when he got to the tenth one, he heard his mother's gentle voice, and saw her face shining from the light of the star, and she said, "You done good, Luke. You done brought these children through. You done real good."

As she finally drifted into sleep, Daylily whispered, "Two more days good walking, and then what we gon do?"

CHAPTER 30

THE MADISONS

Long before they got to the town, they could tell it was going to be different from what they were used to. Harper's Ferry was like nothing they had ever seen before. There were more houses, small farms, animals in the fields and more people than they had seen in a long time.

Daylily had been away from the Riversons' place only to go to other plantations and country houses with her missus. Caswell had never seen a town either. Only Luke had some idea what it might look like from stories people who had been away from the plantation told him. People who had been sold to Massa Higsaw from far away, places like Charleston and Atlanta, told him there were more houses in towns and cities than all the cabins in the quarters and all the outbuildings, kitchens, stables, smokehouses and tobacco sheds put together.

Luke was sure they were close to the town when they started seeing people in wagons. As they saw more and more people, they walked slower and slower. Nobody seemed to notice them. A small White boy in one of the farmyards said, "Hey, y'all." They all spoke back, but they didn't stop.

"How you know we goin the right way?" Daylily asked. "Let's stop and eat something." She sighed and sat down by the side of the road where there was a vacant field. The two boys sat down with her. They were eating the last of the bread Betty had given them.

When they had finished their bread, they walked another half mile. There were times they had to walk up and down the hills, and then there was another farmhouse, and another across the road, and then another. And then they saw a girl about thirteen, hoeing potatoes.

"This here Harper's Ferry?" Luke called out to her.

"Yeah," she called back. "Straight ahead. Y'all not from round here?"

Daylily and Caswell started to say no, but Luke said, "Yeah, we from down the road a piece, other side of the river." And he said it very loud so she couldn't hear Daylily's and Caswell's "no."

Her skin was light brown. She had on a washed gingham dress that used to be red and an old man's jacket over that. Her head was wrapped in a kerchief, and she was barefoot.

"Just keep goin a spell," she nodded. Then she looked at them a little more carefully. "Y'all look real tired. Can I help you to a drink? Mammy's got biscuits from breakfast. That's all we got. What with the war we ain't got much, but y'all just wait a minute. I'll get you some water."

Before Luke could say no, Daylily and Caswell had answered "yes," and she ran off down the path to a whitewashed house with a stone chimney, not too far from where they were standing. Daylily noticed a chopping block.

"I wonder if they got chickens," she said, her mouth watering.

Luke said quickly, "Come on, y'all, let's go."

"No," the younger ones answered together. "We thirsty," said Caswell.

"And hungry," Daylily said and shook her head. "I ain't goin nowhere. So they catch us. They gonna catch us anyway when we gets to that town, and I's tired of runnin."

Luke looked at them, and then back at the little house. "Caswell," he said, "when she come back here, you don't say nothin bout where we from, you hear? And don't tell her no names."

The girl was coming out the door by that time with a jug and something in her hands. Two younger boys came out of the door to stare at the strangers. Luke didn't see any soldiers or White men, so he felt better.

"My Mam say come in and rest a spell," she said, passing out three little biscuits. "That's all we got to offer y'all. Y'all free or slave?"

Caswell said, "Free," Daylily said, "Slave," and Luke said, "Naw, we just tryin to get to Harper's Ferry. We got people there."

"Oh," she said, knowing not to ask any more questions. She looked a little longer at Caswell, and then turned her head away.

"We's free," she said. "My pappy bought us fore he died in the factory makin guns. My name Gracey."

"What's it like," said Daylily, "bein free?"

"Not much different," she said. "Cept we can go where we want to and don't have to carry a pass or nothin. So if we don't make White folks mad or nothin, they leaves us alone. Sides, they say we all free now. Ain't y'all heard of mancipation? Massa Lincoln's paper sayin we's free."

"Who tole you that?" said Luke. "That ain't true, is it?" He thought of Massa Higsaw.

"Sure is," said Gracey.

Luke grinned.

"Can we put some of your water in our canteen? We got to go." Freedom sounded good if it was true, but how could he be sure she knew what she was talking about? This girl was making him more and more nervous. Soon she'd start asking more questions about them. She might get them into trouble.

"Here I'll fill it at the pump, les you want to."

"Thank you," said Luke politely. "I'd be obliged if you would." He didn't want the girl's mother, who was right then peeking out the door, to come any closer and get a good look, especially at Caswell. She had a baby on one hip. Gracey handed him the canteen.

"I thank you," Luke said, "for your kindness." He poked Daylily in the shoulder.

"Thank you, Gracey," she said and poked Caswell, who also said, "I thank you too."

They left the family and soon ran into several more little farms and then buildings bigger than houses with tall smoke-stacks, and lots of men working around them. The river ran right through Harper's Ferry, next to some kind of factory. Their eyes were wide, taking in this new world.

There were not so many workmen on their side of the river, so they were almost alone, but they could see the houses on the hills in the distance. Across the river, everybody they saw seemed to be busy doing something, carrying things like tools or stacks of wood in different directions. Wagons went by, hauling what looked like parts of rifles. They could hear the men shouting at each other.

"Wait now, y'all. We got to talk," said Luke. They sat down on some plank wood on the riverbank. "Now, we don't know what gon happen here. This here's Harper's Ferry for sure, and we got to have a plan. First, Caswell," said Luke, "you know we's colored and you ain't, right?"

Caswell's eyes filled up with tears. "That don't matter no more, Luke," he said. "I thought we was brothers anyway."

"Well, we is, but grown folks don't feel that way about it. They don't know what we done been through. They don't know we's brothers."

"And sisters," added Daylily.

"Right, and sisters," Luke answered. "They just think you White, and we is colored, and that's all they is. Ain't no mixin up with some folks. So we got to remember the plan. If we gets separated, you got to remember. Count on your fingers to ten. Now, every year when them cornstalks get high, it gonna be warm and be summer and then it be harvesttime. And when that happen ten times, hightail it to Betty Strong Foot's before the first frost, so we can be together."

"Luke, that's a powerful long time. We might be dead then," said Daylily. She was about to cry, and so was Caswell.

"You stop that, girl," he said. "You get little Caswell all upset. He ain't but seven year old. Just think about them stars we saw and how we said our mamas be up in Heaven. They up there together, and so we got to stick together too, even if it take ten years. We be grown then. We can do anything we want. In ten summers we gonna meet at Betty's house in the woods, no matter what. When you gets to ten, follow the river back to Betty's house, first time the corn high. Remember, first time the corn is high, then harvesttime. Caswell, count on your fingers too. War'll be over then. Every time y'all look at them stars, think about us, and we'll be together."

Caswell counted to ten on his fingers, and said, "And Luke, I won't forget, your mama is an angel too, OK?"

Luke nodded, and they sat on the riverbank in a heavy silence for a while longer. Finally, Luke said, "Us got to find us some Black folks we can trust."

"Gracey was Black, wasn't she?" Caswell said eagerly. "Let's go. Let's go back there. They had food."

"Yeah, but they had a house full of chirren and nothin but flour and lard," said Luke.

"Maybe they knows somebody though. They's free," Daylily volunteered.

"We need us some Union soldiers, that's what we need," Luke said. "This here might be a reb town."

"Maybe they can tell us then. Let's go back, Luke, please?" Caswell pulled on Luke's coat and started up a chant: "Let's go back, let's go back, let's go back."

Daylily joined him.

Luke didn't have any other plan so he told them, "Yeah, we goin back and ask. Ain't no harm in askin folks." And they turned around.

When they got back to the potato patch, the girl was gone, and Daylily's face fell.

Luke said, "Betcha they in the house. We got to go see. Can't do nothin else."

The girl, Gracey, was out in back of the little house with her brothers and sisters, and her mother was inside with the baby. She came to the open door when they walked up. A dog was barking somewhere near.

"Y'all came back, I see," said the mother. The woman had a pleasant face that used to be round, but she was beanpole thin. She had a turned-up nose and a wide mouth. The baby had dark skin like the mother, and lots of curly hair. She pulled at her mama's ear.

"If you please, ma'am," Luke started. "We just need to ask you . . . somethin happened and we can't find our people."

The woman looked at Caswell a little more carefully. "Who's your people?" she asked, sitting down on the stoop in front of her door. She let the baby crawl all over her.

"Well, ma'am, you see . . . uh, really, all our peoples fighting with the Union, see, and we, uh, we just need to find some Union troops." He sucked in his breath and held it.

The baby wanted to go to Daylily. She stretched out her little arms, and Daylily said, "Can I hold her, ma'am, please?" The woman handed the baby to Daylily. She looked glad for a little break.

"Son," she said, "I see you got a problem here. Where'd y'all come from really? Are you runnin away from somewhere? And where'd you get this little White young'un? Cause I can see the White under all that dirt and sunburn."

"Well, yes, ma'am," Luke said, "I guess you can see that, and ma'am, well, we's just tired. We been runnin and walking, a long, long time. And we just needing somewhere to lay our heads, you see, and some food." Luke sat down on the stoop and put his head in his arms. He cried like a baby in front of everybody. Finally, it was all too much for him, and he couldn't go on any more; he couldn't take one more step.

Daylily and Caswell sat down too, exhausted and past talking. They looked straight ahead, out of reasons, out of questions, even out of fear. There was nothing left to do about anything.

For a few moments, the woman let Luke cry, rubbing him between the shoulders. The rest of the family came out of the house to see what was going on. Then she said, "My name is Iona Madison, and these are my young'uns, Gracey, Zach Jr., Matt, Harriet and Vina. Now y'all tell me who y'all are, and I'll try to help you. That's only fair."

CHAPTER 31

DANGER ON THE STREETS

Mrs. Madison explained to the children that they could stay a while, but they needed to understand that they had to be careful. Union soldiers were all over the place. General Sheridan had taken possession of the entire valley. When the Confederate rebels had been there, it was bad enough, but life for the Madisons and other families was worse than it had ever been, because Sheridan's soldiers had ruined everything they could to keep the rebs from burning it. Bridges were destroyed, crops were burned. Now there was very little to eat and it was dangerous to be out at night. During the day they should not talk to strange men. If anyone came into the yard they were to go immediately into the house. Everywhere there was destruction and suffering. Folks were starving and desperate. But she had to leave the children during the days when she could get work at the hospital, taking dirty laundry home and emptying dangerous slop jars. She was working only because Zach Madison's death had left his family desperate.

The first day Luke and the others were with the Madisons,

Iona had to work in the afternoon. But when she was leaving her hospital job, she ran into some very scary men. She had wrapped her shawl around her to ward off the evening chill. The way home was down a street that had been burned out by Sheridan's men. Now only black skeletons of chimneys and stones rising out of the rubble were left of the buildings. There were piles of charred bricks everywhere.

She had stayed late because there were so many wounded that needed tending to, but she had stayed too late, and she was not comfortable. Iona walked quickly, looking for other people on the street. It was deserted, but she could hear some voices up ahead. As she turned the next corner, she almost bumped into two men who were pushing each other around. She knew they would be trouble as soon as she saw their scrubby faces and snarling mouths.

"Well, well, well," one man said. "Ain't you the lady? Gimme that shawl." He grabbed her shawl before she had a chance to stop him and danced around crazily while the other man laughed.

"They say all nigger gals can dance," the first man said, and did an imitation of a dance with her shawl as a prop. Then the other grabbed Iona and forced her to dance with him. She could smell his foul breath, but she was trying very hard to stay composed because she knew those men would love for her to get hysterical. Somewhere in the distance she heard an ambulance bell and horse's hooves.

Oh, please, let them come by here, she prayed silently. Something had to happen soon or she might not ever see her children again. The men had dragged her into the middle of the intersection and had hold of her arm. Stalling for time, Iona said in a mock polite style, "Gentlemen, could I have my shawl? The night air is a little cool."

They were still standing in the street holding her when suddenly the ambulance wagon was upon them, bells clanging and horses charging ahead furiously. The men let her go to save themselves, and Iona saw her chance. Running for her life, she headed for the edge of town and home.

Luke knew it wouldn't be fair to stay long because the family had so little to eat. The children were all skinny arms and legs, and huge eyes that looked even bigger because they were so thin. They had mostly scraggly winter greens and little pota-toes from the patch out back. How to join up with the Union army was now the main thing on his mind, and he was busy thinking about doing that. That would solve some of the food problems for them, and maybe he could sneak back and bring the rest of them food from the soldiers' supplies.

The family slept in two rooms—the four children in one bed, the mother and baby Vina in the other room. Mrs. Mad-ison made a pallet on the floor for Luke, Caswell and Daylily in the big kitchen Zach Madison had built before he died. The house was the nicest one Luke had ever seen Black folks living in. He hated to leave the house, and it was hard to think about going without Caswell and Daylily. It had real floors, and a big black cookstove, and chairs for everybody to sit in at the table. What he didn't know about were the things Mrs. Mad-ison had traded for food in the last month, precious things she had decided meant nothing next to her children's hunger.

Shortly after dark, Luke lay down with the rest of them, but tired as he was, he didn't sleep well. Union troops pa-trolled the streets. He had seen them yesterday on their way into town. Before first light, he had decided he would go, striking out once more on his own. No one who had known him two months ago when he left his aunt Eugenia as a frightened little boy would have recognized his walk or the look in his eyes. At almost twelve, he was lean and stripped down of the nonsense of boyhood. He would not see Daylily and Caswell again for ten years.

CHAPTER 32

PLAYING SCHOOL

Daylily would not be consoled. She was sure Luke had run off to fight, and, in her mind, to die. She cried for hours as soon as she was convinced that he was really gone. And she was silent for four days. The only time she spoke was to comfort Caswell, who was also in tears when he realized what had happened.

"Come on now, Caswell," she said, her voice low and discouraged. "We can't cry. Luke wouldn't like that; you know he wouldn't."

Iona watched them carefully, this little White boy who looked like an Indian, and Daylily, who seemed to be fiercely protective of him. She had only pieces of their story, and she wondered what had really happened to them. She did her best to make them both feel better, although two more children in a household of six was more than a notion. She didn't say what she thought, that it was a good thing Luke had run off. She'd never have been able to feed him. One thing though, Daylily seemed glad to have a girl close to her age to be friends with, even though Iona would still find her moping and staring at the road after many weeks had gone by. Gracey and Daylily took to each other with relief. Here was a sister to share the load of four younger children, and here was a sister big enough to share girl things with at the end of the day.

Daylily and Gracey had a lot to do while Iona was at work, weeding the garden, trying to appease the younger children, scrubbing the floors. The boys were always hungry, and so Gracey and Daylily were constantly thinking up games for them to play to keep their minds off their stomachs.

"I know," said Daylily one afternoon, "let's play school."

"How we gon play school?" asked Gracey. "We can't read."

"Well, I can," said Daylily. It still surprised her every time she realized that she could admit that without being afraid.

"You joshing me!" Gracey said. "Show me how!"

So Daylily gathered the younger children together to sit in two rows on the ground.

"What we gon write on?" asked Gracey.

"I know," said Daylily, and she ran to the barn, where she had seen some leftover planks of wood. When she returned, she had a piece of flat board and a piece of charred wood in her hand.

The boys were fussing by the time she got back. Vina the baby was playing on the grass, but the girls were patiently waiting.

"You boys," Daylily said. "Get over here and sit down. I'm the leader now." Caswell and Zachary came first.

"Now," said Daylily. "We gon start with ABC."

"What's that," said Zach.

"A the first letter in the alphabet," she answered. "Like if I said, 'A piece of chicken.' A looks like this," and she wrote the letter on the wooden board with her burnt stick.

That day they got through three letters, A, B and C, before the boys refused to sit still any longer, and Zach said, "Oh, shoot, I'm through. I don't care about no ABC."

Matt agreed and school was over for that day.

The weeks went by, and once, returning home from her drudgery at the hospital, Iona walked in on a scene she found remarkable. Daylily was seated in front of all her children except Gracey, reading to them from the family Bible. Gracey was trying to scratch out letters on an old plank with a scrap of charcoal. There was also a child there who lived down the road on a neighboring farm. Because Iona had seen him before and knew who he was, she didn't really worry about his presence. That was, not until much later.

She had never imagined that Daylily, fresh from a plantation, could read and write! Iona was so delighted that she felt a little less tired, a little less in despair that day. And Daylily had found herself at last. From then on, she was one of the Madison family's own, forever.

CHAPTER 33

JAMES JR.

He took his coat and his canteen, that was all. It didn't take him long to get to the center of town. As he was coming close to some ruined buildings, Luke saw one group of Black people and then another. Then on a nearby hill he saw a crowd of Black people clustered around campfires. He decided he'd stop and ask somebody where he could find the soldiers' camp.

The first colored person he saw who seemed really friendly was a white-haired man sitting by the side of the road with what looked like might be his family grouped around him. They were all eating something that looked like bread. And they had a wagon with a mule harnessed to it. Behind them stood burnt-out pieces of buildings and chimneys. There were stones and scorched metal pieces in the road where Luke stood. "Hey, y'all," said Luke. "What y'all doin here?"

"Hey yourself," said the old man. "Who you?"

"I'm Luke," he answered.

"Don't have no last name?"

"Guess it's Higsaw," said Luke. He wasn't quite sure what

the rules were about names now that he had run away from Massa Higsaw.

"Guess it is, then," said the old man. "I be John Miller. We been following the federal lines. My son, James, he just gone looking for the soldiers to find work. This my grandson, James Jr." He pointed to a big boy who looked to be about fifteen.

Luke said, "Hey."

"Hey yourself," said James Jr. He had on an old felt hat, and some overalls and a jacket. He was barefoot and he was really heavy and tall.

"Which way he go?" said Luke, excited now that he was so close to the troops.

"Yonder, up that hill," the old man pointed. "See them colored folks? Go up there, and right over that next hill there'll be soldiers' camps. You want a piece of hardtack?"

"Thank y'all," said Luke.

"We got that following behind soldiers. They be dropping things, leavin they old things behind."

James looked at Luke. "You goin up there?" he said.

"Uh huh," Luke said while trying to chew the stuff. It was the hardest thing he had ever tried to bite. "Goin to join up," he said.

"Wait," said James. "Let it go soft in your mouth first. Then chew it."

James moved closer to Luke. "I wanna go, Grandpapa. Just wanna look. I ain't goin to join up."

One of the women spoke up. "You don't need to go runnin off. You just get in trouble. Let this boy go on bout his business." She had a toddling child who was pulling at her hand.

"Please, Mam, I's tired sittin here," he said.

She looked at him, too weary to say no. "Gwan" was all she said, and waved him on with her hand.

Luke and James Jr. walked off toward the hill up ahead. Luke looked up at James Jr. "How old are you?" he asked.

"I be fourteen next year," James said. "How bout you?"

"I be twelve soon. Don't know what month."

A small company of soldiers went by, and the boys stood still and watched. As they started walking again, the conversation turned to guns, rifles and soldiers.

"Had me a rifle once," Luke boasted.

"Naw, that ain't true, you ain't had no rifle."

Luke protested, "Yeah, I did."

"Where'd you get it then? You lying."

Luke grinned. "Stole it from ole Massa."

"Where is it then?" James said.

"Lost it when I was captured."

"You better stop your lying. You ain't been captured!"

"Yeah I was," said Luke, swaggering just a little.

James wasn't giving up. "Where then?"

"Back there where I come from. I was captured before the battle."

"What battle? You ain't fought in no battle!"

"Yeah, I have. One where the captain got his face blowed off."

"You need to stop lying," said James. "God don't like no lying."

Soon the town got busier and busier with the bustle of the military activity and wounded soldiers, distracting Luke and James from the question-and-answer game. They saw supply wagons filled with large bags of grain. Even a skinny cow wandered by.

James's eye was caught by a wagon with no driver. A mule was hitched to the wagon, but no one was watching it. It was filled with apples and other foodstuffs. "I sure could eat one of them apples," James said to Luke.

"Not yours for the taking," Luke said. He didn't want any trouble, not from the soldiers, not from the police.

James was determined. "You done took a rifle from a White man. How you gon tell me about stealing? Lookee, there's a hundred apples. So many you wouldn't miss just one! And I'm really hungry. We ain't had nothing but hardtack to eat all day!"

"This is different," said Luke.

"How different?" said James.

"I don't know. Just is. Not yours, James Jr. Leave it alone," Luke said, a warning in his voice.

But by the time Luke had finished the word *alone*, James Jr. was across the road and had reached into the covered wagon. Luke cut out running fast and hid behind the corner of one of the few buildings left standing on the battle-scarred street. He dared a quick look from around the corner of the building. Suddenly he heard a man's voice cry out, "Halt!"

The man was a ways away, but he was pointing his gun at James. When the big boy looked up, his right hand was in the apples and his left hand was reaching for another one to stuff into his bib overalls. When the shot rang out, the look on James's face was not fear, but surprise, and then he crumpled to the ground. His body shook a little and was still.

CHAPTER 34

A DEATH IN THE FAMILY

They shot him! Luke thought, for taking some apples! He was just hungry and they shot him! It wasn't fair. It wasn't right! Luke's whole body was shaking. He tried to focus on the eagle Betty had said was in his spirit. The eagle is with me, he thought, the eagle is always with me. He was afraid to show himself, and he heard running in the street. He didn't know what to do. Then he heard a voice say, "Come get this dead nigger! Dadblasted contraband nigger! Get this baggage out of the street!" A pig on the loose squealed and ran down the street.

Luke leaned against the wall where he was hiding. He was so scared, his teeth were chattering. He had been with James. What if they took him to jail? Or shot him too? He bent over with one hand on each of his elbows. He could feel the tears on his face, but he was mad, not sad. Angry that someone could get shot dead for being hungry, and taking some apples. Angry that James had been following him and now he was dead. He stepped out from behind the corner just in time to see them drag James's body away like a sack of potatoes.

Luke felt like it was his fault. If he hadn't been trying to get to the campground, James would still be alive. Maybe there was nothing special about him after all, Luke thought, and nothing special about the eagle spirit either. Maybe Betty was wrong, and the eagle was just a dumb bird. It didn't help him save James Jr. Luke swiped at his tears with his coat sleeve.

He swore to God that one day he would pay James Jr. back. He was gonna fight for the Union to help end the war, and when he grew up, he was gonna do something to help colored people, so they could be treated better, so they wouldn't be so hungry they had to steal apples. He didn't know how to help yet, but he would find a way.

Luke sat there next to that wall until the sun was low in the sky. He was trying to decide if he should go back and find the Millers. What if they blamed him for James's death? Luke felt more alone than he ever had. He wanted Betty to tell him what to do, but she was far away. This was hard. It was worse than taking a whole bottle of Aunt Eugenia's spring tonic. He didn't want to go back, but there was no help for it. The Millers would be waiting for James Jr. to return.

It took him just a few minutes to get back. He saw the Millers' wagon with a sinking heart. He had been hoping they would not be there, but there they were. James's grandfather was asleep in the wagon. His mother sat with the toddler. Luke wished James's father had come back and he could tell the father instead of the mother.

James's mother looked at him over the wagon railing. "Where James Jr.?" she said.

"Well, uh, ma'am, it's been some trouble," Luke stammered. He put his hands in his trouser pockets, then took them out.

"I knew it! He done got himself arrested or something worse!"

"No, ma'am," Luke said, looking at his feet. "No, ma'am, he got shot."

"My Lord in Heaven!" She stood up, holding on to the side of the wagon. "He dead?"

"Yes, ma'am," Luke whispered.

Her cries woke up the grandfather, who started yelling, "What rebel killed my grandson. What rebel?"

The other woman was wailing now also. Luke stayed with them until they calmed down a little and told them the soldiers had James's body, but there was nothing more he could do to help.

"I'm going now, ma'am," he said, "and ma'am, I sure hope y'all have some good luck and I sure am sorry." In a few more minutes he turned and walked away, saddened and tired.

CHAPTER 35

BOSTON

As he made his way back near to where James had been shot, Luke noticed that the people on the hill had started lighting little fires. At least there was food there, and maybe he could get warm. Nervous but determined, he started out toward the campground. Once he had passed by the colored people who were following the troops, it was close to sundown. One of the soldiers on watch saw him. "Boy," he said, "ain't you Captain Fields's boy?"

Something told Luke he should say yes. It was easier and maybe safer than saying who he was.

"Here," said the soldier. "Take this note to Lieutenant Percy. Just ask up there on the ridge. Somebody'll point you in the right direction."

Luke was glad to have something official to do. That way if someone asked him what he was doing there, he could say he was on an errand for Captain Fields. He started toward the area the soldier had pointed to.

Although he had to ask two more men where he could find Lieutenant Percy's tent, he was finally successful, finding the lieutenant, who seemed glad to see him, or at least re-

lieved to get the paper Luke was carrying. He smiled when
he saw Luke.

"Come on in," he said, "and have a cup of water. You
must have walked a long way." He pointed to a dipper and a
bucket of water while he read the note. After he read it, he
seemed satisfied. "You might as well curl up there for the
night," he said. "I'll not bother with an answer. What's your
name, boy?"

Luke hung the dipper back on the bucket. "Luke, sir."

"You look exhausted," said the soldier. "If you are hungry,
there might be some beans left in that can."

Lieutenant Percy was short, and his uniform looked a bit
too large, like he might have lost some weight during the war.
He had dark, almost black, hair, and was clean shaven. What
impressed Luke the most was that he seemed to be a kind man
who had a nice smile.

Grateful for a bite to eat, Luke ate greedily and went to lie
down on the dirt floor to sleep, thinking about how he might
persuade Percy to give him some work to earn his keep. But he
didn't have to worry about that.

With the morning, Percy seemed to find it convenient that
Luke was there, and glad for the help. He kept asking Luke
to do things, run errands, clean and order the lieutenant's
space.

That afternoon, Luke even managed to cook a rough
supper.

"You mighty handy, boy," said the lieutenant. "Is Fields
expecting you back? You have anywhere to go now?"

"No, sir," said Luke. So that was it. In exchange for his
meals he got to stay and even earn a few coins. He worked
hard, but Luke liked Percy and Percy liked Luke, and so all the

rest of that year Luke was in the thick of the war, working for Percy, even carrying water to wounded soldiers. Sometimes it was exciting and sometimes it was very dangerous.

Lieutenant Percy also put him to work watering the horses. That had to be done twice a day, after reveille and once in the afternoon, and there was always more than enough to do when it came to caring for the animals, and never enough men. Boston was Luke's favorite horse. He belonged to the lieutenant and had been born in Massachusetts. Except for his two front white ankles, the horse was all black. Boston was an artillery horse. That meant he had very dangerous work to do on the battlefield, pulling the caissons and the battery wagons.

One morning Luke was giving Boston the last piece of sugar he had taken from the lieutenant's supplies, and Boston was nuzzling his face as if to say thank you, when the bugle sounded "to arms." Luke jumped.

Someone yelled, "Boy, move your behind!"

Luke got out of the way fast so that the horse could be harnessed up to the battery wagon he was pulling. He ran to get his water bucket. Wounded soldiers would soon be needing him.

It didn't look good. They were taking a beating. Soldiers were soon dragging the wounded as far out of the line of fire as they could and leaving them there where the medics could get to them. When they called, Luke would carry his bucket of water to them.

He ran out of water and went to fill his bucket a second time. The deafening sounds of guns, dying men, and shrieking, whinnying horses made it hard for him to hear what the men were saying. He got down on his knees so he could give one man a sip of water and hear him.

The soldier moaned, and as Luke leaned over him, he said weakly, "Son, what are you doing out here? You ain't big as . . . a roasted peanut." He coughed fiercely and blood came pouring out of his mouth before he could take a sip of water.

"I'm sorry, sir," said Luke. "I don't have anything I can clean you up with."

But the soldier was almost gone. "Tell em," he strained to say, "tell em I did good . . ."

His head fell back into the grass. Luke couldn't linger. He knew war now. He knew that one man's death wouldn't stop a battle. He could hear the screeches of horses being shot by the enemy. Not Boston, he thought, please not Boston. He couldn't stop. He had to go on to the next one crying for water. He kept looking over his shoulder to see if he could get a glimpse of Boston, but it was impossible to see anything clearly in the smoke and confusion.

When the bugle sounded the rally, he knew they had won the skirmish. Soon those left alive were piling up the dead men and horses to be buried. He got his bucket and headed for the makeshift stable to look for Boston. For an hour he helped water and comfort the exhausted horses. But there was no sign of the black horse with the white ankles. Luke gave up and began to make his way back to the lieutenant's tent. He was dirty and heartsick. He felt like he had lost another friend.

Convinced Boston was dead, he was hanging his head and walking slowly when the lieutenant saw him.

"Son, you look mighty low," he said. "Don't you know our boys won this thing?"

Luke looked up and there was Boston alive and well, stand-ing right next to Lieutenant Percy. He was covered in mud, and blood splattered, but he was alive.

"He got separated out there and found his way back to us," said Percy. "I was just going to walk to the stables to have him cleaned up, but here, I guess you'd like to do that."

Luke smiled for the first time that day. "Yes, sir," he said gleefully. "Thank you, sir!"

CHAPTER 36

VICTORY

Surrender came in April 1865, when he was twelve. Luke would never forget it because it was the last battle Lieutenant Percy was in, and Luke was wounded in the leg.

Percy was up and dressed as usual by five o'clock in the morning. He seemed somehow lighthearted to Luke, not like a man going into battle.

"Luke," he said, "this war's about to be over. We got them on the run for sure now. Do you know what that means, Luke? You'll grow up a free man. Won't that be fine?" He put his cap on and fastened on his sword. "You stay out of the fray today," he said. "Don't want you getting hurt. I plan to hire you and pay you a real wage when we get back to civilization." He left the tent on his way to rally the boys to "fight a good fight," and Luke wondered if Percy meant he wasn't supposed to carry water that day. Finally, he decided to get out there and do his job. Besides, he wanted to keep his eye on Boston.

In the middle of the battle, Luke was racing along a white picket fence that bordered farmland next to the battleground. Confederate soldiers were beginning to jump the fence. The Union had them beating a retreat and they were running all through the pastureland, stumbling and frantic. Luke was going in the opposite direction, carrying the water bucket. The whole world seemed to be exploding around him. The Southern soldiers didn't even notice him.

In all the uproar he didn't hear it coming. The bullet hit him in the leg. Suddenly his leg collapsed and he was down, yelling and writhing behind a dead horse and a broken caisson, in more pain than he had ever endured.

He woke up in the hospital tent, waiting for the surgeon to sew up his wound, and somebody said, "Here, boy, take a drink of whiskey, it'll help the pain." He was swallowing whiskey for the first time. It was burning all the way down into his stomach when a private came bursting into the hospital tent and screamed, "It's finally over! The war's over! The South surrendered! We whupped em, boys, we whupped em! Wooeeee!! Hooray for the Union, hooray for the Union!" And all the sick soldiers who could holler did, and Luke thought how glad he was that he had helped the Union win, even a little bit, and he smiled, and then he heard men running and yelling, and that's all Luke remembered, because he passed out when they started sewing up his leg.

CHAPTER 37

SCHOOL

It was 1867. The war had been over for two years. Still, life in Harper's Ferry wasn't all that easy. One Saturday morning Daylily woke up early. This was the day she was going into town with Mama Iona, and she was excited. It was her turn to go. They had to get some supplies. They only went to the general store once in a great while, after Mama Iona had saved up enough pennies to get a few things. They had not been to the store for three months and were out of coffee, flour and salt. The children begged and prayed she'd bring back a little bag of sugar for treats. She didn't promise.

Daylily poured a little water from the pitcher and washed up in the washbasin. She put on a clean shift. The sun was just barely up and they had to walk to town. The walk took about an hour, but it wasn't too long for Daylily. She loved being out in the sun, seeing all the people.

Iona called her softly, "Daylily, you up?"

"Yes, ma'am," she answered. "You gon wake the young'uns?"

"No, Caswell and Gracey know what to do."

The walk to the store took them past farms and cow pastures. Soon they began to see buildings that had not yet been repaired and rebuilt from the fierce battles that had taken place in Harper's Ferry, dark burnt-out chimneys, and tumbled-down bricks, and a few other early travelers. Saturday was everybody's day to take care of their families' supplies. There were a few wagons too, drawn by mules and horses. Soon folks started waving. "Morning," they would say.

Iona and Daylily waved back even when they didn't know the folks. "Mornin to you," they said. In some places they saw crews of men working on buildings.

When they finally got there, the general store was crowded. There was a line of folks getting chewing tobacco, and another line for yard goods, another one for tools and another one for seed. Daylily looked at the cloth on the shelves and thought she had never seen such pretty cloth in all her life. Her favorite was the blue covered in little white forget-me-nots, but she knew better than to ask for it. They would never have enough money for that!

"Let's come back later," Iona said. "Too many folks in here. I got business at the Freedmen's Bureau anyway."

"Yes, ma'am," said Daylily, wondering what the Freedman's Bureau was. They headed toward a little white building that said "African Methodist Episcopal Church." A sign that said Colored Welcome was tacked on the door.

"Thought we was going to that Freedmen's place," said Daylily.

"This is where they said to come," Iona answered. Inside, large windows let in the sunlight. A Black man in uniform was sitting behind the biggest table Daylily had ever seen. He told Iona to have a seat in a chair facing him. Daylily stood next to her. Afraid to stare, she looked out of the big window. The man handed Iona some papers to fill out. When she hesitated, he said, "Ma'am? Can I read it for you?"

"I can write my name, sir, and I knows just a few words."

"It's all right," he said. "I can fill these out for you."

He asked her a lot of questions like how many children she had, when and how her husband died, and where she worked, and how much money she made. When he put the papers aside, he looked at Daylily. "Little miss," he said, "do you go to school?" His voice was loud and deep, and when he spoke to her, she jumped. Iona looked at her as if to say, Answer the man.

"No, sir," she said in barely a whisper. She fiddled with her dress sleeve. It made her nervous to have to answer the soldier. She thought about Caswell back at the house. She knew he wasn't really supposed to be with them, because he was White, and she wondered why Mama Iona had counted him when the man asked her how many children she had. Daylily was worried there would be trouble and then Caswell would have to leave and she would never see him again like she might never see Luke. Once when Mama Iona took Daylily to church, someone asked her how many children she had "adopted." After that they didn't go to church very much.

The soldier's booming voice rang out again. "Do you know about the Freedman's School, ma'am?"

"I don't have much money, sir," she said.

Daylily noticed he had on a pair of glasses. Not many folks she had seen wore glasses. "It's free," he said, looking up at Iona from his chair.

She was standing up now, ready to go. "Your children can go to school there, and you too if you want. See Mr. Fielding in room number two. This little girl can go to school now that the war's over. That's what we fought for, you know." He wasn't mean, he was just loud.

"Yes, sir, thank you, I'll see to it directly." They walked out the front door and then Iona stopped on the front steps. The street was busy with men hauling bricks and wood in the bright sunshine. Iona was thinking. She wrinkled up her forehead.

Daylily was silent. She was trying not to show how disappointed she was that they had not gone to room number two to see that Mr. Fielding. She wanted to go to school more than anything. She had dreamed of it, and she was afraid to even think it could come true.

Iona saw Daylily looking "down in the mouth," as her husband, Zach, used to say.

"Honey," she said, "do you want schoolin?"

Daylily couldn't even answer. She just nodded. Her mind was racing all over the place. Mama Iona needed her at home. Of course she did. It would never happen. It wouldn't be fair to Gracey, who was four years older than her and was Mama Iona's blood child. Of course she would be the one to go first. Maybe they wouldn't take but one child from each family anyway, and maybe . . .

Betty had said she was like a mama bear, always teaching her cubs something. Maybe if she got some schooling, someday she could teach somebody else besides Caswell, Zach Jr., Gracey and the others. "Words be God's voice," Granny had said. "Teach folks to read the words." But then her heart sank. Who would help Gracey watch the young'uns while she was at school? Iona had to work or they would all starve.

"I can't," she finally blurted out. "Who gonna watch the young'uns all day? Gracey can't do everything by herself."

Iona's mouth was set. "Let's go back in and ask. Must be some way. Caswell's ten now and the baby is three. She can drink out of a cup. Caswell can watch them."

"He can't go to school?" Daylily asked.

Iona shook her head. "You know the reason," she said.

She could come to class twice a week. Most everybody who signed up had to work; folks had their crops and houses to rebuild, and they needed their children to help. There were lots of folks who wanted to learn, old and young, and the Bureau tried to make it possible. They said she could come on Monday and Wednesday, and stay all morning. Iona signed up Gracey for Tuesday and Thursday.

Daylily woke that Monday feeling good and bad. She thought that Caswell should be in school too, but there was nothing she could do. The night before, she and Caswell had been outside pumping water for Iona to wash up after supper. He was holding a bucket, but he didn't look too happy about it, or about anything.

It took the water a while to come up. "Hurry up, gal," he said. "I'm tired standin here." His forehead was set in a frown.

"What you all riled up about?" she said.

"Nothin, just go on, work the pump."

"I know," she said, looking him in the eye. "You mad. You riled cause I'm going to school and you can't go."

"No, that is not true."

"Yeah, it is! You know why you can't go!"

"Yeah."

"Listen, I promise. I'll teach you everything. Everything

I learn, I'll teach you, and then it'll be just like you was there, OK?"

Caswell turned and went into the house without a word.

Daylily kept her promise, faithfully tutoring Caswell the best she could. She tried to make him feel better about not being able to go to school, but he wouldn't talk about it much except to say he thought it was a "real stupid thing."

That little room at the Methodist church was Heaven for Daylily. Iona would walk with her halfway, and then turn off to go to her job while Daylily continued on the road to the church where classes were held. Her teacher's name was Miss Elizabeth Rowell. She was White and young and Northern. They sat in straight rows and recited the alphabet, all of them together, old and young. The oldest person there was an eighty-year-old man.

The first day Miss Rowell made them say why they wanted to be there. She said the younger ones needed to know how important it was to be able to read. Everything was so exciting to her that Daylily forgot to miss Luke so much, but she was still sad about Caswell. She prayed for Luke and Caswell every night like Granny had taught her.

Then something happened that scared all of them at home. Miss Rowell came to their house. One day, about two months after she had started attending school, Daylily was in the back-yard helping with the washing. They were boiling water for washing dirty clothes in a big black kettle. Daylily was hang-ing clothes on the line and practicing her spelling in her head. She happened to look down the road and saw a horse and buggy coming their way. Miss Rowell was driving. "Mama," she said to Iona, "here come Miz Rowell."

Iona dropped the petticoat she was washing into the black kettle of hot water. "Gracey," she said, "run tell Caswell to hide in the shed, now! Quick!"

Miss Rowell stopped the buggy in front of the house and got down. She was knocking on the door at the same time Caswell got to the shed. Iona walked through the house and went to the front door, wiping the soap off her hands. Her eyes were bright and tense. Daylily was right behind her.

"How do, ma'am," Iona said when she opened the door. "Come on in. Ain't you Miz Rowell from the school?"

Daylily said, "How do, ma'am."

"Well, hello, Mrs. Madison. Daylily, so nice to see you."

"Won't you sit down, ma'am? I was doin my washing. Sorry I ain't more presentable."

The teacher looked around for a chair. She was a short, plump woman with bright pink cheeks and mouse-brown hair that was parted in the middle and slicked down on either side. She had on a long brown and white gingham dress. Iona motioned to the chair usually reserved for Iona or for company. It had a stuffed embroidered seat. Iona sat in a little wooden chair by the front door. There was still very little furniture in the house.

Iona turned around and noticed Gracey wasn't there. She said, "Daylily, go get Gracey to say hello to Miz Rowell."

"But it's Daylily I came about," said Miss Rowell.

Daylily got hot and cold all at once. What had she done wrong? Would they take her out of school? Her eyes filled with tears.

"Now, it's nothing to worry about, Daylily," said Miss Rowell. "The truth is you are doing very well, and I just stopped by to encourage you, and to tell you the Freedmen's

Bureau is very impressed with you. They want to make sure you don't stop coming to school. They think someday you could be a teacher and help teach your people when you grow up. There are many, many colored people who need to learn, many more than we can serve here, and we need your people to train them, so we want to be sure you are studying, because you are one of the brightest pupils in the school."

Daylily was smiling all over now. Even her dimples were showing. "Thank you, ma'am," Iona said. "We real proud of our Daylily. Daylily, say thank you."

"Thank you, Miz Rowell," said Daylily. "I do love school."

Iona looked toward the kitchen. "Daylily, get Miz Rowell a cool cup of water from the pump. And tell Gracey to come in and say hello to our company."

On her way to the pump, Daylily heard Miss Rowell say, "How many children do you have, Mrs. Madison?"

Oh, Lordy, thought Daylily, let her remember not to count Caswell. She heard Iona say, "Six. I have six, ma'am." Her schooling was safe unless Miss Rowell found out about him, and then none of them knew what would happen. She just couldn't lose her chance to get more schooling. She even had her own book now, called *The Freedmen's Spelling Book*. More than anything she wanted other people to know what her granny said. "The words, the words be God's voice. Make you free."

Gracey was standing by the back door. "What she want?" she said under her breath.

Daylily mouthed silently, "Where is Caswell?"

Gracey pointed to the shed. "What she want?" she said under her breath.

Daylily headed to the pump. "Tell you later. Mama say come in and say hello."

Gracey made a face, but she went inside. Daylily got the water and took it to her teacher. Miss Rowell left soon afterward, and nothing else exciting happened that day. That would come later.

CHAPTER 38

HIDING OUT

After Gracey warned him, Caswell had run to the shed and shut the door. The shed was made with small logs, and light came through the open spaces. He could peek out and see what was happening without being seen. The girls' teacher Miss Rowell was in the house.

He got used to the dark quickly and looked around at Zach Madison's farm tools, at least those Iona had not sold during the lean times when the family did not have enough to eat. She had kept two rakes, two hoes and a shovel. There was an old mule harness hanging on the wall. The shed smelled faintly of manure and old feed sacks.

Caswell sat on the ground and peeked through a chink in the shed. He didn't see anyone but Gracey, who was watching the younger ones, Matt, Harriet, Zach and Vina. They were running around playing some game; he didn't know what it was. He could hear Matt protesting about something.

He didn't like this hiding. What if he was caught? Would he be punished like his papa's slaves were? He remembered hearing about a slave on the home place who was a runaway, and had finally been brought back. He was little then, and in the kitchen, underfoot with the women, Gran Susie, and Bett the cook and others. They were talking as if he wasn't there about a captured slave who had almost made it to free- dom. "Hid out in the wilderness for forty days and nights like Jesus," said Bett. "Just like Jesus in the wilderness. Mir- acle he wasn't dead when they found him."

"Well, he be dead tomorrow or near dead when they finish with him," said Gran Susie.

Caswell remembered those words *hid out like Jesus*. He thought how awful it would be to hide in the swamp for days. At least when he was with Daylily and Luke, they were in the woods and not a nasty swamp. He didn't like this hiding, and it wasn't fair that just because he was White, he couldn't go to school with Daylily and Gracey. It felt like he was being punished for being White like the runaway slave was for being Black. When he grew up, he was going to stop hiding. He was going to school, and he was going to find out why Jesus was hiding in the wilderness. He thought Jesus was White. He wanted to learn, and he wanted the whole world to stop this Black-White thing. It just made life messed up all the time.

Betty had said he was a pathfinder. Well, he wanted to find a path where he could be free and so could everybody else. All the pictures of Jesus that he remembered were White. Was he like Caswell? Was he being punished for something that wasn't fair? Mama Iona didn't take them to church, but she prayed all the time.

He looked through the crack and saw Matt, Harriet, Zach and little Vina still playing with Gracey. When the school- teacher lady left, he was going to ask Mama Iona why Jesus was being punished and hiding out. Suddenly he heard the back door squeak. He looked through the hole again. Daylily pointed to the shed and then Gracey went into the house. He sat very still and watched. In a few minutes, Mama Iona came out, and Gracey came to fetch him.

CHAPTER 39

STEPMOTHER

Somewhere between the bloody finish of the war and the rise of the Klan, Caswell's father had married again, and moved to South Carolina. The new Mrs. Washington was older, smarter, and a better judge of character than Caswell's mother had been. The war had hardened her as it had hardened them all.

Mrs. Troy Washington looked up from her work at the table in the kitchen. She had heard him coming. She always knew when he was in the house because he had been wounded in the war, and walked with a cane. Shelling peas was something that would have been done by the darkies ten years ago, she thought. Now her hands were much less softened by beauty oils, when she could manage to get some, and she thought of this rather than hearing the voice of her husband.

"I'm off to fetch my son," he had said. "The federal troops have located him with the help of some concerned citizens, friends of mine, and some scared niggers who were willing to talk."

The word *son* went out of her mind because she wanted it to. She had a way of not hearing what she didn't want to face.

She pushed back her light brown hair that tended to come undone when she was working in the kitchen. She looked up at her husband, who was beginning to have a middle-age spread but was still a good-looking man.

"What, my dear?" she said, picking at another pea shell.

"You could at least listen when your husband is talking," he said. "A matter like this should not be unimportant to you. My *son*. I have found my son, who has been stolen by some nigger woman in Harper's Ferry, I'm told. He should be thirteen by now. His mother was Loddy Washington, with whom you are not unfamiliar."

Matilda thought, How could I not know who he was talking about, since he insists on comparing me with her as if she were some paragon of virtue, or some dead saint. But she bit her tongue.

"I intend to retrieve him and restore him to his rightful place as my heir," Troy said. The word *heir* was what made the word *son* real to her. Her head snapped upright like one of the pea shells she was breaking open, and the peas in her hand rolled onto the floor.

"I leave in a few minutes. See that you have his room ready by our return, and try to instruct that Negress you're *paying* to treat Master Washington with the respect that he is due. He's nearing manhood, and sorely in need of a White man's discipline, I'll warrant. His mother was a lady and I expect the same example from you. He was seven when she died. He will remember. I will be gone for about two weeks. Once I rescue my son, I have business to take care of in North Carolina."

He strode from the room, leaving her alone. Her emotions were restrained by an instinct for self-preservation. Troy was a cruel man whose need to control was as large as his appetites were. A question from her would be interpreted as a challenge to his authority. Better to add this to the long list of his other traits she had accepted since their marriage began.

There was no convenient place to put this affront to her expectations. Her entire reason for marrying Troy had been security and his ability to hold on to at least some of his fortune after the war. True, much of his money was gone, lost to the Yankee greed that in her mind was the whole reason for the war. He was still considered prosperous by any standard. But now there was a son in the picture, a White son, unlike the others. She could only guess at how many niggers he had fathered.

Matilda heard the squawking of a chicken being pursued by Lina with the ax, the capture, and then the thud of the ax against the chopping block. The maid, Lina, would have to be told. Matilda would not have her maid thinking she had found out about Troy's son on the same day Lina was informed.

Lina opened the back door and took the large black kettle off the hearth she used to boil water before plucking chicken feathers. "Scuse me," she said quietly.

"Lina," said Matilda, pretending that this was old news, "have I ever told you that Captain Washington has a son by his first wife?"

Lina, a former slave, concealed her surprise. "No, ma'am," she said in an almost imperceptible whisper, and without turning around.

She knew her place, this Lina. Hear no evil, see no evil. But Matilda knew that White people never really knew what their servants were thinking. Their impudence was as hidden as her real attitude was toward her husband, and why not, thought Matilda; we all have to live the best way we can.

"He'll be here in two weeks. See that you have the upstairs guest room ready for the young master."

"Yes, ma'am," Lina murmured. She closed the door quietly behind her. The dead chicken's blood stuck to the doorknob, to her hands and skirt. She went to the pump with the large pot, filled it with water, and put it on a fire she had built out behind the kitchen.

Matilda rose and went to her room. There was no hurry with the peas. Troy would not be there for dinner at any rate.

CHAPTER 40

FOUND

Captain Troy Washington was seething with anger at those he had owned, "cared for" and even fathered. He was never reconciled to the outcome of the war. God had turned his back on the Confederacy, and Troy had turned his back on God. His rage was full and overflowing. And so by the time he reached Harper's Ferry, there was no way to contain it.

The approach to Iona's house was through the town, and then he had to travel on a rather sparsely populated road that led to the house, so he could be seen coming from a distance. All the children were in the house. Daylily was looking through the window to see if the rain had let up so they could go outside, when she saw a man approaching.

"Mama Iona," she said, "there's a rider coming down the road. He a White man."

Iona looked through the window. A White man stopping at their house could mean only two things: either someone she owed money to, or something she didn't want to think about— Caswell had been discovered.

He was close enough now that they could tell he was clearly coming to their house. She knew who he was. There was no mistaking his resemblance to Caswell. Her heart sank like a stone.

"Quick," she said to the children. "Y'all go into the kitchen. Now!"

The children scrambled, aware there was danger, not sure why. Daylily had seen the man and knew it was a serious threat.

Caswell whispered in her ear, "Who is it?"

"I don't know," she whispered back. "A White man."

Although perfectly in order and clean to a fault, Iona's house was only a nigger house to him. A nigger house with a nigger criminal raising his son. He had put both the Klan and the army on to searching for the boy who just seemed to have vanished into the war. They had looked in North Carolina and Virginia in all of the major cities, and finally after six years they had found him in Harper's Ferry. Now Troy was here, and he was determined to have what was his.

Troy Washington ordered Iona to open the door, and she did so with a look of one whose life has suddenly turned into a calamity.

"You know why I'm here," he barked at her. "Where is he? I know you have him. Your so-called neighbor down the road has heard you calling him in for supper. 'Caswell,' you hollered, and they told my people in order to save their skins."

Iona did not bother to deny the truth. The child who came for reading lessons that day and then came back often to play must have said something to his folks. She couldn't expect to keep a child away from his kin forever. Besides, she had the others to think about. The night riders were fearful and violent. They were confederates who were mad about losing the war. They hated colored people. She knew what they could do. If she resisted, there would be hell to pay. Her only hope to save the other children and herself was to cooperate.

"Caswell, come here, honey," she said, her eyes red with the effort not to cry. Caswell, now a tall, lanky thirteen-year-old, appeared from a side room. Their similarity was very clear. There were the same gray eyes of Troy Washington looking at her from Caswell's face. There was no mistaking it. In spite of Caswell's well-tanned face and long hair, in spite of his rough farm clothes and calloused hands.

Caswell had taken one look at his father and known him instantly. Now he only looked at the floor in a numb disbelief. How had this happened? In one second his life had been torn apart, never to be put back together.

Daylily was standing in the shadows, her mouth open in horror. She shook with fear, wringing her hands and twisting her white apron so hard she almost ripped it. And she was afraid to look, afraid Washington would hit Iona or take her away. Nineteen-year-old Gracey was holding a screaming six-year-old Vina by the hand.

Well, let them wail, thought Troy Washington. "You wench," he said roughly, grabbing Iona's arm. "By rights I ought to turn you out, or better yet give you to the White man's law. Do you know who I am, nigger? Do you know what they do to niggers who steal children?"

Troy grabbed Caswell's face by the chin and turned it to the right, looking for the scar on his son's ear. There was no way he could miss it.

Daylily let go of her apron and covered her mouth in horror. Caswell opened his mouth to protest, and Troy slapped Iona once on each cheek. Gracey let out a cry, but Iona was silent. The other children stood helplessly in a corner. Finally, Caswell couldn't stand it.

"If you *are* my father," said Caswell, "you'll listen. She took care of me real good! She gave me a home. I wasn't scared no more, and I had somebody to be with. You don't know what we went through in the war. You don't know!"

"Shut up!" Troy yelled. "Shut up!"

Caswell plunged on, stammering. "But it wasn't her fault. I was the one who wanted to stay! I was. We couldn't find you!"

Troy spat on the clean floor. "Makes me sick to think about it!" He walked toward Caswell and grabbed him by the nape of the neck. Troy yanked Caswell toward the door, and then he fixed his eyes on his son. "If you so much as mention their names to me again, I'll come back here and burn them alive. Do you hear me? And you sluts," he said, looking at Iona, Gracey and Daylily, "you tell anybody about this, anybody, you mention this boy's name to anyone alive, you're dead."

As he dragged Caswell out of the house, the boy stopped protesting. Somehow, he knew it would go harder for Mama Iona if he made his father any angrier. He went quietly, a lamb to the slaughter. He would hold in the grief and the outrage, but he would have his life. One day, he would be in charge of his own life. He would stop hiding, and he would come back and make things better for his family, Daylily, Mama Iona, and all the rest of them. He would have his own life; he had paid dearly for it.

CHAPTER 41

TO BE A WHITE MAN

His stepmother didn't make his life unbearable, not all by herself. It was bad enough to have lost his "family," but even more terrible was hearing his father's voice and the constant ridicule and hatred for people he had loved and who had loved him. On the other hand, his stepmother seemed to think he was something strange and alien, because he had been raised by a "darky woman." She hated his habit of treating Lina like a friend, and kept telling his father he needed to "take that boy in hand" and teach him who he was.

"There is no reason to talk to darkies, unless you are giving orders," she told him time and time again. She told Troy the boy was withdrawn and stubborn, and that he still talked like a nigger, making mistakes in his grammar. But his father, who could be hard enough on Caswell himself, would not tolerate any criticism of him from Matilda. The lessons of what it meant to be the White man who ruled by God's decree would be entirely under Troy's control.

Matilda and Troy often had guests. Entertaining was one of the few things they both enjoyed. After-dinner smokes meant arguments among the men only, about Reconstruction and politics, but mostly about hatred. Caswell had to hear comments like, "It's 1870; they been free for five years. Five years too long, I say." His father's friends puffed on their cigars, and as the smoke permeated the carpets and their clothes, they continued to express their hatred.

"We shoulda burnt that nigger too like we did the other one," one man said. "Down in Mississippi they don't just burn em, you know, and they make the family watch."

Choking on the smoke, Caswell coughed roughly.

"What's ailing you, boy?" said his father, slapping him on the back. "Smoke's good. Make a man of you." All the men laughed.

Troy said, "They are getting out of hand, I tell you, thinking they should dress and even live like White folks."

Caswell nodded, pretending that he agreed, because he was afraid to defy his father, even while he was seeing Daylily's and Luke's faces in his mind.

On the other hand, Caswell wanted more than anything in the world to please his father and be one of those cigar-smoking Southern gentlemen. He wished he could make his father smile.

For a while when he was fourteen, he even wanted to become a member of the Ku Klux Klan and wear a disguise. But then, just as he thought he could do that and be a good son to his father, and fit in and be accepted, he would remember his sister Daylily and his brother Luke, and Betty Strong Foot, and Mama Iona, the only mothers he had known after his mother died.

When he was fifteen, and the war had been over for eight years, he tried to talk to his father about Luke and Daylily. Caswell had just come back from a ride. He put his horse,

Strong Foot, in the stable, and went through the house to the library. He found Troy on the veranda. His father had his back to the library door, looking over his cropland.

"Daddy," Caswell said, "I need to speak with you."

Troy said, as if he had not heard his son, "I've got to get more profit out of these crops. We didn't make enough this year."

Caswell continued. "Daddy, I want to tell you about my time away with Luke and the rest." Caswell wanted to tell him about their long walk from North Carolina to Harper's Ferry, and about how they had become like brothers and sisters. "You don't understand," he said quietly. "If you knew them, if you would just listen to me, you'd know they're people, just like you and me."

Troy turned around so fast he almost lost his balance.

Caswell would never forget the look in his father's eyes. It was like looking into gray ice. Immediately, he knew he had made a terrible mistake by saying they were just like Luke and the others. Troy gripped his cane, and Caswell looked away from his father's face. His eyes focused on his father's large knuckles, almost white, he held the cane so tightly.

"Now you listen to me, boy, and you listen well." He wasn't shouting, but there was something in his low-pitched voice that was much worse than shouting. "Niggers are not like us and they never will be. Niggers are animals. And like my horse and mule they were put on earth to be servants to the White man. Do not ever, ever let me hear you say that they are like you and me again. Or, and I promise you this on my father's grave, I will beat you with this cane until the blood runs."

Troy walked into the house, and Caswell could hear the

cane and the man's footsteps going through the parlor and up the stairs. He listened until the terrible sounds faded away, but he could still hear his father's voice in his head and see his enraged eyes. He had listened to his father, and he had listened well, and he would never forget what his father said, because that was when he realized he was still hiding, hiding who he really was from his father and his father's world, and hiding sometimes even from himself.

He thought about Betty saying he had the spirit of a wolf inside him. Betty had said, "The wolf is wise and leads others, especially his own family." Caswell knew his skin was white, and he was not an Indian and he was not Black, but in his heart he was just a person. At that moment, he knew that the truth was that all people were sisters and brothers. He had to find out what to do with this feeling that was so strong in him. He wanted to know more about what was in the Bible.

Caswell used to go to church with his mother every Sunday, and he'd heard about Jesus saying, "Love one another." And He had never said anything about not loving people who were not White. So Caswell stood on the veranda and let the tears run down his face and over his chin. And he wept for his sister and his brother, and for Betty Strong Foot and for Mama Iona, and was not ashamed.

CHAPTER 42

DECISION 1874

And then the day came. The day when he was forced to choose. He awoke to the peace of Indian summer in Charleston, South Carolina. Hot sun shone through the curtains of his bedroom. October, still hot in South Carolina.

Lina knocked on his door with the news that breakfast was ready in the dining room. She always let him sleep as long as possible. She seemed glad to have him around the house, and he would always regret that he had not been able to say goodbye to her.

He heard only the early morning seabirds that had come into shore looking for food. Until he splashed water from the basin in his room on his face, he heard only those peaceful sounds. And then there were horses, and men talking to his father in hushed and excited tones right under his window.

Caswell was halfway through his breakfast before his father came to the table. Troy sat down to his coffee, and Caswell recognized the anger he had seen so often.

"Damn niggers have to be brought to their senses," he said. "There's only one way to teach them who's in charge. They don't listen to anyone." Troy reached for the preserves. Matilda quickly excused herself, even though she was not through eating, knowing things were going to be said that Troy didn't allow her to hear, and that he would have sent her out of the room had she not left.

Caswell chewed slowly. He didn't dare ask what had happened.

"I want you there tonight," said his father. "You're seventeen now. It's time. The boys are all getting together. We'll put those niggers in their place. After dark, nine thirty. This'll be a good education for you."

Caswell asked to be excused. Suddenly he wasn't hungry any more. There was little point in protesting or even making up an excuse for tonight. Troy had already made up his mind.

It was a very long day for Caswell. He spent most of it pretending to read, but really worrying about what was to come.

There were ten of them. The moon slid through the trees, making the white robes stand out in the night and the shadows more sinister than usual. Caswell felt the tension in the men and in his own body.

Some of the men carried unlit torches. There were two groups. One for the death, one for the burning.

"The nigger refused to pay, and then he disputed me," one of the men said, in between chewing furiously on his tobacco. "He called me a liar. No nigger should get away with that and live!" He spit his chewing tobacco as far as he could.

The closer they got to the man's house, the worse Caswell felt. They were really going through with this thing. He stepped on a twig in the dark.

"Hush up, boy!" one of them said. "Surprise is the big

thing." This man was a friend of his father's, someone he knew.

Suddenly they stopped walking and each man put on a white robe and a hood, so Caswell could see only their eyes. He wasn't sure which one was his father now, or his father's friend. In the darkness an owl was disturbed from his gloomy perch and flew up into the night with a great flutter. Caswell's stomach turned over. He had no robe and no hood. He was to observe, to learn, they had said. He was told to stay in the background at the edge of the clearing, out of sight.

All of them surrounded the pitiful little cabin this family called home, ghastly men in deathly white in the dark. Suddenly a gun was fired. Someone lit the torches.

"Come on out here, nigger," one of the men in white said. "Come on out and git your punishment! We'll teach you to think you can talk back to a White man in South Carolina." A Black man came to the door. He had brought a lantern with him. Caswell could see by the light that the man was frozen with fear.

"Please leave my family alone," the man begged. "They didn't do nothin."

"Do we have to come in there and git your woman too?" The men were closing in toward the house.

The man stepped out onto the ground, and they surrounded him, dragging him deeper into the woods. Caswell heard the whimper of a child, and then somehow a torch was lit and thrown at the cabin. He heard the Black man screaming as smoke and flames leapt into the air. Caswell didn't know exactly what they would do to the Black man, but he knew that whatever it was, it would end with the man's death.

They had surrounded the Black man and started pulling his

clothes off. Caswell lost his sense of who was doing what; white robes were everywhere. There was one scream of agony. Suddenly, Caswell felt like he was in one half of the world and those men in the robes were in the other half. Caswell could not see what the men were doing, but when he saw a flash of metal, he knew that they were cutting and slashing the Black man's body. He ran forward into the horrific noise. "Stop it! Stop it! Please stop it!" Caswell screamed. In the torch-light, he could see red stains on the white robes. No one heard him. No one even remembered that he was there. The men were in their own world of noise and blood and unleashed hatred.

When he looked up, the Black man was hanging from a tree and blood was everywhere, dripping from his naked body. The white-robed men were rejoicing, slapping each other on the back, laughing, screaming, pulling out their flasks. They were way past seeing Caswell. In the orange light from the fire, Caswell lost his dinner, and then, beyond knowing the sound of his own sobbing, beyond knowing which white apparition was his father, he ran through the darkness, intent only on reaching his horse and leaving his father's house forever.

CHAPTER 43

RUNAWAY

He rode hard for miles. When he realized he was not being followed, he stopped to rest his horse. The long days of childhood travel had taught him much about sleeping in the woods and finding his way. He was closer to North Carolina by now, but Virginia was three days away. As his horse rested, he thought. He made his plans.

He knew he'd never be able to go back home again. He smiled a sad smile and thought, I'm a runaway for sure now. Just like the captured slave I remember from my childhood. But I'm not about to hide out in the swamp, he thought. I'm going to find Daylily and Luke, and then, I'm going somewhere I can learn about love. There must be other people like me, who understand that this hatred has to stop. Suddenly it occurred to him. Seminary, he thought, that's where people learn about God. That's where I should go.

He would have to find some kind of work. To save money so he could pay for his training to become a clergyman. He had no friends in this part of the country. His horse pawed the ground, restless, defiant. That horse had been his only real friend all these lonely years. He had named him Strong Foot without telling his father why.

Just then, Strong Foot seemed to be trying to say something to his rider, and then Caswell began to listen to the countryside, the sun just rising, the dried cornstalk on his left. Ten years, the tenth summer, and harvesttime . . . before the first frost.

"This is it," he said to his horse. "This is the day." The horse turned toward the north and Virginia, and Caswell gave the bay his head. They were free.

CHAPTER 44

THE TENTH
SUMMER, 1874

Daylily hadn't thought about the tenth summer for a long while, at least not consciously. But she thought about Luke and Caswell every day in one way or another. She hadn't thought that three, then four, then five years had gone by, but she wondered every day whether Luke was dead or not. Had he made it through the war alive and whole? And what had happened to Caswell? Would he still call her his sister?

She wondered whenever she saw a running stream or the stars in the night sky, or ate fresh rabbit meat, or cooked a stew like Betty Strong Foot had taught her. She wondered if they would ever see each other again. Life with Mama Iona was good, and God had given her a whole new family, an education, and a wonderful job teaching her people how to read, children and old people who were eager to learn.

If she thought back all the way, she'd marvel at how she used to sneak to read just because she was Black, and how Granny almost died from a beating because she was teaching people to read. Knowing Granny's sacrifice made Daylily more and more determined to teach for the rest of her life.

She still had her little skirt and jacket Betty had made out of Confederate uniforms. At first, when she got way too big for it, she let Vina Madison wear it, but after that she put it away to keep. It was the one thing she had from that time that would bring it all back as if it had happened yesterday. It was a small reminder of Betty's cabin, Betty's love, and it brought Luke and Caswell very close to her. She kept it in a cedar trunk that Mama Iona refused to trade for food, because it had been made by Zach's own hands.

There came a day, then, that brought her up short. It was early October. Corn in Virginia had been harvested. They were making ready for the first frost. One day out of many others when there was something special in the air, in the way the sun shone off the dried cornstalks as she walked to the schoolhouse. In the smoke from someone's stovepipe, she smelled breakfast.

But this day, she didn't think about how to divide her ham and biscuit between those children who didn't have any lunch, or about whether the school could pay her next term. She thought about how many years it had been since that day they had walked into Harper's Ferry. Ten summers. It had really been ten summers, and now it was early fall. She realized with a start that it was time to go. She would set out in the morning.

CHAPTER 45

BEFORE THE FIRST FROST, 1874

Luke had worked for Percy until he was seventeen, and then he told the retired lieutenant that he had found work that would give him a better chance at life. He wanted a skill, and he could work in the railroad yard. He did not want to be a servant for the rest of his life, but he didn't want to say that to Percy. They had parted as friends, and Luke would always be grateful to Percy.

As Luke walked down the street in Winchester, Virginia, he noticed three children walking together. They touched his heart. He never saw children without remembering. He never got through a day, really, that something didn't remind him of Daylily's giggle and Caswell's natural stubbornness. He still carried sadness with him that he had not been able to say good-bye to them ten years ago. And he carried a pain in his left leg from the skirmish he had been in. One pain kind of brought the other one, always reminding him of what he had left behind in his youth.

But his limp was the last thing people noticed when he stood up to speak on the race question. His voice was strong, and his spirit was even stronger. He knew the war had been kind to him. He had seen enough battle to know that, even in one year. Others who were left living had missing parts and worse.

Luke had no bitterness about his wound. He was glad he had been able to help bring freedom, if only in a small way, and the wound was a symbol of that. Every time he thought of those days with Daylily and Caswell, he thought how much he would love to tell them about what he had done when he left the Madisons'. About how he had become a water boy for the Union troops, carrying water under fire, until he was shot in the leg. He wondered if they were still there with Mrs. Madison or if they had been split up by White folks.

This morning he was excited. He had learned that Frederick Douglass was coming to Richmond to speak. Luke planned to be there in the front row, learning everything he could about how to help in the struggle for complete freedom. Things were really bad these days, White folks were angrier than ever, and something called the KKK had taken the place of the overseer's lash.

He was on his way to work. And he was lucky. Colored didn't have much to pick from. They got the last jobs. Luke was working at the railroad yard, lifting and hauling railroad ties to help with the rebuilding. He limped, but that didn't keep him from being strong enough to be a good worker. In his heart, he knew his real work was freedom building, and he carried a kind of light with him that other people couldn't understand but followed anyway. He knew he had this light and he counted it a gift, a second sight almost. He carried with him always the memory of Aunt Eugenia and his mama, Betty Strong Foot, Daylily and Caswell. What he did, he did as much for them as for those to come.

All at once, he noticed that the children he had seen were going in the same direction he was. Two boys and a girl. And then he remembered. Ten summers. The tenth summer was here. The corn was already harvested, and it was time. They had not had a cold snap yet.

He couldn't let them down. He had to be there. If he hitched a ride on the way to Harper's Ferry, he could walk the rest of the way. Work would have to wait. And Mr. Douglass would have to wait. He had made a promise to Daylily that he wouldn't get killed, and he had to keep that promise.

CHAPTER 46

REUNION

As he felt his way through the woods, following the river and dodging low hanging branches, Caswell couldn't help feeling excited. It still amazed him that they had all survived that ten days in the woods and all their adventures at Betty's. He had been a baby, really, and the others weren't much more.

He was the first to arrive. His heart sank when he didn't see anyone as he approached the cabin. Suppose they had forgotten? Or maybe Luke did go off and get himself killed, and maybe Daylily grew up and forgot both of them. Maybe she was married and had a house full of children and a husband who wouldn't let her come. As he thought about it, he was sure that's why she wasn't there. Of course she'd be married. Who wouldn't want Daylily for a wife, and what kind of husband would have her running out to the wilderness to meet two men?

His horse picked its way carefully up to the front of what he was sure was Betty's cabin. Although slightly overgrown, it was almost exactly the same as he remembered it, only it looked even smaller because he was so much bigger. A few vines had begun to cover the sides of the log house. Betty's little chair that she kept by the door where she went to smoke was still there. Yaller Feet wasn't there, but his lean-to had almost collapsed, and the garden was completely overgrown with weeds. If Betty was inside, he didn't want to startle her. He dismounted and tied Strong Foot to a tree, speaking softly and petting his horse's nose. It is as quiet as death here, he thought. A robin began a song, and the sun went behind a cloud. No dogs barked a warning. He remembered when Yaller Feet and Pretty Boy were stolen.

"Betty?" he said, knocking softly. "Betty? You home?" The door wasn't latched. He pushed on it and it opened slowly. Caswell looked around carefully. He didn't want to surprise anybody, especially when he thought about the squatters that could be there using Betty's cabin. He stepped all the way inside, and his first thought was that everything was so small. It couldn't have been that small ten years ago.

And his second thought was that nothing had changed. It was all in place. Even the boxes that said "U.S. Provisions" and "Confederate Issue" were still there, but they were empty. He touched the ashes looking for warmth, but the hearth was cold. She had not been here last night, he guessed. Caswell sat down at the table where he had eaten so many meals for two months, and a great sadness flooded his heart. He had not once thought of the possibility that Betty could be dead, and he had not noticed the message for him lying on the table.

Luke would come, he thought. If he was alive, Luke would not let them down. Caswell got a book from his saddle-bag, gave his horse some water from the river and settled in to wait.

• • •

It was late that evening when Luke walked up to the cabin he recognized as Betty's. Intense memories crowded his mind in a rush. Tastes and smells and feelings all muddled into one. When he saw the horse tied outside the cabin, he was full of anticipation. At least one of them had remembered, unless Betty had got herself a horse.

Strong Foot whinnied, and then Caswell heard him. He went to the cabin's door, not sure what to expect, and saw Luke standing ten feet away.

"My God, you tall, boy!" was Luke's greeting. "You been growing like a weed or what, little brother?"

Caswell grinned, and Luke laughed out loud. They embraced as brothers, and for a minute there was a deep quiet between them as they felt the wonder of seeing each other again.

Luke broke the silence. "And you look right White too! Haircut and real boots! You ain't been out in the sun lately!"

Caswell threw back his head and laughed. "Look at you," he said. "Ain't you a sight for sore eyes! All muscled up and clean-cut. Looking like a gentleman!"

"I'll be a monkey's uncle if you didn't remember!" Luke said, laughing again. They punched each other on the shoulder in the way men do when they really want to cry. "Daylily here?"

"No, not yet," said Caswell, "but don't give up hope; you know how women are, always late!" They laughed again as if every movement, every word was a delight.

"Betty?" Luke asked in a more serious tone. He knew the possibilities. He had seen the war up close. Betty was living a dangerous life, and now he knew just how dangerous. Caswell shook his head.

"No Betty."

They went inside the cabin and shut the door. Since it was near dark, they lit a candle. Caswell had a fire going. He had found a stack of small logs by the fireplace and a good amount of provisions, some dried meat and fish and some dried fruit. They talked themselves into the wee hours, sharing plans and ambitions, Caswell's hope to become a clergyman and Luke's to become a political activist. Times were bad. It seemed as one war got over, another, trickier one had started. It didn't look good for Black people and freedom.

Things had been kept up inside the cabin. It was clean, somebody had swept all the cobwebs away recently, and Betty's pots were mostly in place. Luke saw a feather and a small wolf carving on the table, but it didn't really surprise him. He was so focused on the reunion that he didn't pay any attention to the small objects. He just remembered that Betty always had Indian stuff around. The quilts were clean, and it was almost as if Betty had been expecting them somehow, although she knew nothing about their plans to have a reunion. After talking until the wee hours, they finally fell asleep on the old pallets.

CHAPTER 47

HARVEST

At seven o'clock that same morning, Daylily had started out for Betty's cabin. She wore walking shoes and her teaching dress. Mama Iona knew where she was going and why, but she worried anyhow. Sure that it wasn't good for a woman to be alone, she begged Daylily to use their mule and ride in the wagon, with the boys Zach Jr. and Matt.

Finally, Daylily gave in and said they could go, because she knew it would take at least twenty-four hours or more to get to Betty's, even with the mule, but she said they couldn't go all the way up to the cabin. She couldn't explain it to them, but she had to do it alone.

Iona knew that this was something that belonged only to those who had survived it. It was only right for Daylily to be alone. Those three had kept each other alive. This belonged only to them.

About a quarter mile away from Betty's cabin, Daylily said, "Y'all go on back now. Mama said wait till the sun moves a quarter of the way down the sky. If I ain't hollered out, I'm there safe, and y'all can go home."

She hugged them both and started out walking for the cabin. "I'll be fine. Just follow the river back home. My brothers will see me home." The youngsters settled in to wait, and Daylily disappeared around a bend in the river road.

As soon as she saw the horse, she realized she was nervous. It had been a long time since they were children. She was a grown woman now. Luke was a man. How would they feel, remembering all those things they did as children? Luke knew her better than anybody else in the world. He had seen her close to death, in despair, and half naked and desperate. And Caswell, she was suddenly realizing, was a young White man. In her memory, he would always be the little boy she had come to love, who had almost become Black, but now, today, it would be different.

Luke and Caswell heard or felt her approach, and opened the door. A young woman stood there like an angel in the woods, graceful, slim and dressed in blue gingham with a white lace collar. For a flash of a minute, they thought she was someone else. She had never been so beautiful. And then her face melted into the little girl with the dimples they remembered. They all stood face to face.

"My brothers," she whispered. "Y'all are my brothers, y'all are the reason I'm alive today." Her eyes got full, and all her shyness was gone in the embrace of the two young men who would always be her first family.

The day was spent in more talk, more sharing, and a lot of laughter, remembering how clumsy Luke was with a fishing pole, and how comical Caswell looked in his coffee-face disguise. Daylily and Luke each said where they were living, making sure they would never be out of touch for too long. Caswell shared what had happened to him at home, and he vowed to write as soon as he got settled.

As the afternoon shadows grew longer, they sat around catching up, wondering, talking, and thinking about Betty, loving and missing her. They were all thinking the same thing, each unwilling to conjure up what they felt might be true.

Daylily had brought a present for Betty, a new sewing kit, needles and thread in a leather case. Caswell went outside and dug a wonderful new pocketknife out of his saddlebag that he had brought for Betty, and Luke's gift was seeds, melon, cucumber, and sunflower.

As she laid her gift down, Daylily noticed three objects on Betty's little table—a bear claw, the carving of a wolf and an eagle feather. "Look, y'all, have you seen these?"

"Oh, yeah. What are you thinking?" Luke answered.

"Luke, I'm thinking she left those for us. Don't you remember? She used to call us Gray Wolf, Little Bear and Blue Eagle. Don't y'all see? She's tryin to tell us something."

Caswell fingered the wolf carved in wood. The wolf spirit, she had said, is courage, loyalty and faithfulness. His job is to keep the family together and share good medicine.

"She told me I am like the mother bear," Daylily whispered. "Fierce and protective of the young. Like my granny, a teacher of the way. 'Old Mother Bear knows things,' Betty would say."

"I don't believe she gave me this," said Luke. "Do y'all know how special an eagle feather is? You can get one only if you are a shaman, a healer. This was her mother's. One day she told me her father left it to her because he didn't have no sons. She was holdin it for her son or . . ." His voice trailed off. He was overcome.

"She is tellin me I have to become a great healer of the people, and lift them up," he said quietly. "She has faith in me to do this." His voice cracked with emotion.

"I thought the eagle had let me down," he said, shaking his head. "But I was so wrong. I understand now. If Betty left me this, it means I *am* the eagle. I am supposed to help lead our people to freedom."

They were all very quiet, lost in their thoughts of the past, realizing that Betty had believed in all of them, and had seen the lives they would lead. Luke lit the lamp and put it on the table. They sat around it silently, thinking and just being with their memories of Betty.

Finally, Caswell said, "Is there anything else around here? Anything to tell us where she is? Any clues?"

There was an old blanket hanging on the wall to keep out drafts over the place where they used to sleep. It caught Daylily's eye, and she began to really look at it for the first time.

Caswell noticed her staring. He was puzzled by her expression. "Daylily, do you see something? What is it?"

She shook her head. "That old blanket that was always there? She was working on it while we were here. There's a picture in it I never noticed before. The threads are so much the same colors you can hardly make it out. I thought I saw . . . yes, see? There's an eagle there. And over there a . . . yes, it's a bear and . . ."

"A wolf," said Caswell.

They were silent.

Then Luke said, "It's a message. It's us, woven together to look like one thing, but if you look good . . ."

"It's everyone," said Daylily. "Everyone different and the same. Like she used to say, the Great Spirit don't care what color you are or what color the angels are."

"Should we take it with us, I wonder?" said Caswell.

"No, she might need it," Luke said.

Daylily shook her head. "She's gone," she said quietly. She was fingering her bear claw. "She's gone. She won't be back."

"You mean dead?" Luke looked up from his feather.

"I don't know. Maybe, maybe not. But she's left here. She's finished with this place. She only left enough food for our visit and blankets for us to sleep on. Didn't you notice? She knew we were coming. But she's gone. She won't be back. You know Betty and her ways. Haven't y'all felt it? I felt it, almost as soon as I got here."

"I was afraid of something like that," said Luke. "I just didn't want to say it out loud."

Caswell silently agreed.

They sat around the lamp a long time, savoring their memories, knowing it would be some time before they would be together again. Luke would be traveling. He was going to get a job with a Black uplift organization, and Caswell would be up North in some seminary. He didn't know how he'd pay for it, but he vowed to them he'd find a way. Daylily thought she'd keep on teaching where she was, at least for a while. The presence of Betty was even stronger than it had been earlier in the day. They knew that wherever she was, she was with them.

Luke remembered that frightening night he had to go on a spy mission and say, "Red is dead. Sunrise on the left," and sing "John Brown's Body," and so they all sang "John Brown's Body" and laughed at how scared he was when the tall Black man with the beard rose up in the cornfield.

He could laugh about it now, but that battle was a close call. And then they all cried when once again he shared the battle experience that had made him a man.

Daylily sang, "Mama, Are There Any Angels Black Like Me?" and she taught it to them, and she told them she taught all her students that they were angels.

They had great fun teasing Caswell about how dark he got, and how folks didn't know what he was. Finally, it was time to sleep. They put the pallets down where they had always been, under the blanket. Daylily took off her shoes and asked them to turn around while she slipped out of her dress, although it made little sense to her, since they had already seen much more than her underwear many times. But they did it anyway.

Luke built a small fire to take the chill off. They opened the door and took a look at the darkness of the woods and autumn stars, and then they were in for the night.

"Frost coming," Luke said quietly as they barred the door. And then Caswell saw something they had missed. "What's that in the corner?" he said. It was an old gray scaly thing.

"A snake skin," said Daylily. "A rattlesnake skin."

"Been there a while," Luke said. "Snakes shed in the spring, not the fall."

"Not there by accident," Daylily said. "She put it there for us. Betty told me all those years ago, snake skins are a sign of new beginnings. It's a sign of new life. Time for us to go on without her, and do what we supposed to do."

In the morning, they decided to leave their gifts to Betty on the table as a way of thanking her and as an offering to the Great Spirit in her name. They left the blanket on the wall to speak for Betty. And if any traveler came by and used their gifts, well, she would have liked that more than anything.

ACKNOWLEDGMENTS

Special thanks to my family, those living and those in Spirit, for all their great love, support and energy. Thanks for cheering me on about this book when the going got rough and the road was long.

Special thanks to all of my dear sister-friends who never tire of giving me the inspiration, time and attention needed to persevere. Thanks for never losing faith in me or in my Black angels.

Special thanks to my dear friend Gabrielle Beard, who was there for me when I had lost the courage to try again.

Special thanks to those who came before, ancestors unknown, who lived the struggles that made it possible to tell this story.

I appreciate the longtime assistance of my agent, Marie Dutton Brown, who continues to affirm that I can do this work; my wise friend Cheryl D. Woodruff, who gave much advice; and my editor, Stacey Barney, for her outstanding professionalism and her tenacious belief in the project.

And finally, to the Mother-Father of us all, Deo Gratias.

356740S0S06675

CHASE BRANCH LIBRARY
17731 W. SEVEN MILE RD.
DETROIT, MI 48235
578-8002